Love

Outside

The

Boundaries

By

Sandra L. Wyllie

Dedication Page

I dedicate this book to my son Austin. He experienced all of this first-hand. I am sorry that he had to go through what he did. He's a smart and determined young man who is in college now.

I would like to say that not every therapist abuses patients. There are many good ones out there. I hope that this book doesn't discourage people from seeking psychological help. I also wish that professionals that still carry their own wounds to get help themselves. Look for the red flags, like too much physical touch and self-disclosure.

I want to thank my husband for helping me format this book. I have no computer knowledge. He got this book up and running. I also want to thank him for hanging there with me, and putting up with all my shit. Another man would have left me a long time ago.

Contents

Chapter 1 – I'm A Borderline

Let me introduce myself. My name is Sandra or Sandy, if you prefer and I'm a borderline. I never actually knew that until I hit my forties, and then that Madonna song "Borderline" took on a whole new meaning for me. Actually what could one expect being raised by a very abusive narcissistic mother and a paranoid schizophrenic father that was in and out of mental hospitals all his life.

I was an only child growing up in a suburb of Boston and kept to myself most of the time. I blocked out a big chunk of my childhood the years my parents separated. This was when I was between the ages two and five years old. I was living with my mother then, although daddy would visit every weekend. I was severely abused at this time by my mother. She would lock me out of the house for hours. One time I wanted to come in so bad that I banged my head clear through the glass door on the porch. Shards of glass shattered all around a fragile little girls head. She grabbed a hold of me and beat me so hard with a spatula that left large welts on my bottom.

My mother always had special names to call me like cock-sucker, or fucking whore. I never knew how she could call a virgin a whore. But she hated sex. I was close to my father, though. When he was on his medication he was very caring, not affectionate with hugs or kisses, but gentle and kind. He would often go to the race tract and would take me with him time to time. We would also go to the beach and out to dinner a lot. More than anything he would listen to me hours upon end.

That was daddy "on his medication". Daddy off his medication was an entirely different story. He was a mad man, a raving psychotic lunatic. He would put the fear of Jesus into me that people were trying to kill us. He made me afraid of my own shadow. He said we couldn't eat because the food was poisoned. But the saddest, most heartbreaking part of all is he denounced me as his daughter, saying I was some byproduct of my mother's adulterous affair with my cousin Johnny (daddy's nephew).

I never dated in high-school. Except for three close girlfriends I predominantly kept to myself. I went to an all-girl catholic school overrun by nuns. Because of this I started having crushes on the two male teachers there, Mr. Mollard and Mr. Sullen. I got a hold of Mr. Mollard's number in the teachers' lounge and called him one night. He asked how I got his number I said "I went into the teachers" lounge. He asked how I got in there. I said "I walked in". Yeah I was a bit nuts back then too, taking risks. I remember stapling the pages of my Latin teacher's book together. I loved to do crazy pranks and was voted zooiest. What does that tell you?

I never did socialize like the other girls. I never went to dances or my prom. I was painfully shy and had a severe anxiety disorder and also social phobia. The panic attacks were real bad. Back then I didn't know what was really happening to me. I thought I was dying. I couldn't breathe at all and I use to get severe dizzy spells that I believed I had a brain tumor. My aunt died of a brain tumor in her fifties, so I thought that must be what I had. Oh, yeah did I mention I was a hypochondriac?

I wanted to go away for college and got accepted to Notre Dame, a Roman Catholic college in New Hampshire. But my mother discouraged me (as always) so I ended up in a community college in Wellesley. I took up Early Childhood Education and got my first job as a pre-school teacher at the local YMCA'S preschool. And here at Massachusetts Bay Community College is where I met my first boyfriend who later became my husband. We were both virgins.

When I met Andrew (the man I married) I was eighteen, almost nineteen. I had never even been kissed by a boy and I was greener than the grass in Ireland. I thought he was "nice" but there was no real attraction. I knew I was getting on in years and if I turned him down who else would want me? My mother put the fear of Jesus in me to marry and not have sin, (sex) before then. So that's what I ended up doing marrying Andrew at the tender age of twenty-two.

My parents owned a two family house and when I married they kicked out the tenants upstairs so Andrew and I could move in. That was in September 1987. That way my mother still had total control over me. At this time I left my job at the YMCA and went to work at Stone & Webster Engineering in Boston as an administrative assistant. Andrew was working there as well and got me in. I started developing crushes on the older men who worked there. There was just no "spark" in my own marriage.

At the age of twenty-seven I went off the birth-control pill and started trying to get pregnant. I knew I was going to have trouble because I didn't ovulate often and sometimes I would go months without getting my period. And indeed I was right! I couldn't get pregnant, which began the roller-coaster ride of fertility treatments and doctors. At first they put me on a low dose of clomiphene. It worked well. I got pregnant but that pregnancy ended in a miscarriage. At this time I lost my job, was gaining a ton of weight and sinking into a deep depression over the miscarriage.

The doctors kept putting me on higher doses of clomiphene, which, at this point wasn't working at all. Ironically clomiphene was introduced to suppress ovulation but instead it had the opposite effect and woman got pregnant on it. My sister-in-law got pregnant with twins taking clomiphene. With me it had the effect that it was originally supposed to, that is, it prevented pregnancy. So then they tried IUI's (intrauterine insemination) where they treat my husband's sperm and inseminate it into my uterus. But that didn't work either. So I just gave up and was told by doctors I would never get pregnant. Two months later I finally got pregnant on my own with Alex, after two years of trying. What do doctors know!!

It was a very sad time around Alex's birth in the summer of 1995. My dad was mentally regressing and neither of my parents went to Alex's baptism. Andrew lost his job, and I wasn't working. We had to turn to welfare for help. I felt isolated and all alone and at this point. I didn't have any female friends to turn to either.

Eventually Andrew landed a job doing phone support for Microsoft. He was trying to get into the field of developer/programmer after going to night school at North Eastern. He had to work night shifts and I was very much alone. Even though my parents both lived downstairs in the same house my dad was in seriously bad shape and I wasn't talking to my mother. The only thing that soothed me was breast-feeding. I lost eighty-five pounds and was trying my best to get myself back together.

When Alex turned eighteen months I wanted to have a second child. We both said we wanted two children. Ironically we wanted girls but I ended up having another boy –Austin in December of 1997. No, not after Austin Powers or the state of Texas, or even my mother –in-laws maiden name (which was Austin) ....just Austin. After Austin was born we started noticing changes in Alex. Something wasn't quite right with him. His pediatrician set us up with a doctor at Children's Hospital and that is when we learned Alex was autistic.

It was devastating at first and I felt overwhelmed. I had a new baby, an autistic toddler and a schizophrenic father who was regressing. Also at this time my marriage was rapidly going down-hill. I hate to admit this but I started losing patience with Alex. He was a very difficult to deal with and I was so unhappy. I started living on the internet and looking for men. I had never been with anyone except for my husband and I didn't feel in love with him at all. I was curious about what it would be like to be with another man.

I developed a relationship with a man that I met on the internet. Randy was unhappily married as well. He also had two children (girls) and him and his wife were also virgins when they married at the tender age of nineteen. We had a lot in common. He was a kook like me. He was a rather large man and I was a very small, petite girl. He was the only sexual experience (at that point) I had other than Andrew. It was a whirl-wind relationship of sex, hotels, New York, sex, fine restaurants, sex, roses, sex, gold and gemstones, sex. Did I mention sex?

At the time I was seeing Randy, Andrew and I were barely talking. Then when one morning my whole world shattered and fell apart. It was April of 2000. Alex had a bad cold and Andrew took him to see the pediatrician the night before while I stayed home with Austin. The doctor put him on antibiotics and he went to bed early that night. The next morning we woke up we found Alex in a comma in his bed, stiff as a board with his eyes rolled back in his head, unresponsive. We immediately dialed 911.

This is how your whole life can turn on a dime. Alex was rushed to Children's Hospital with acute meningitis/encephalitis in a comma. It was on Good Friday he went into the coma and Easter he opened his eyes for the first time. He was hooked up to everything in the ICU, a tube for his urine, a tube to feed him, a tube in his arm for medication. I think I just shut down completely. He spent two weeks at Children's Hospital in Boston. Doctors said he might never recover. He had severe brain damaged from his illness. They told us it was a one in a million chance of an autistic child being struck down also with meningitis/encephalitis.

Alex was transferred from Children's to Franciscan's in Brighton, a rehabilitation hospital where he lived for the next two years. I would visit him every day from early morning to early evening, just like having a full-time job to go to. There Alex had to learn everything over again, from eating and drinking on his own, to walking and even speech. He kept having seizures and was put on several different medications, which they had to keep altering because he had a severe allergic reaction to some of them.

When Alex regained his strength he was put into an enclosed netted bed that zippered all around and kept in a wheelchair all day, NOT because he couldn't walk but because the illness caused Alex to have no impulse control. I didn't know this child any longer. He grunted like an animal, would eat his shit and regurgitate and had violent outbursts. One day I walked into his room in the hospital and his diaper was off, his shit was smeared all over his bed and he was jumping and wailing like a baboon. It was truly heartbreaking to see. It was then we knew Alex would never live at home again. We had lost our first born and Austin would be raised as if he was an only child. Austin has no memory of Alex living at home. He was only two years old when Alex got sick.

Since Alex couldn't live at home we had to start looking into residential schools for him. He had recovered all he could physically at Franciscan's and now he needed emotional and educational help. He had extremely limited language and no impulse control and was still in diapers at six years old. We looked into a few programs, one was at the Boston Higashi School for autism. But now Alex had much more than just autism. He had severe brain damage as well. We finally came up with The May Institute and Alex moved to his new home, outside of the hospital where he had been staying for the last two years.

At this time a very dear minister that I was exceptionally close to got thrown out of our church. I grew up a catholic but married a protestant man. I 'll never forget all the help Weldon gave us and his sage words which ring so true "where there is love there is deep pain". Before Weldon left he said I should get psychological help. He set me up with my first psychologist Dr. Beth Guild.

She was in Norwood. We also started seeing Weldon's good friend for marriage counselling. I had never been in therapy before, although I needed it. I was thirty-eight and on a new journey, a psychological one that would change who I am for the rest of my life.

A lot else was happening around this time too. I lost both my parents back to back. My dad was diagnosed with terminal liver cancer while he was staying at Mclean's Hospital for his schizophrenia and my mother suddenly died from cardiac arrest. I remember having to tell dad two painful things, first that his wife had died and second that he himself had only months to live. He did not believe doctors. Now we had lost three people in our household, my parents and my son. My mother died the day after Thanksgiving in 2003 and my father followed suit in February 2004.

I met my best friend Holly at the park around this time. She had just given birth to her second child prematurely and he was still staying at the Brigham and Woman's. So although she lived in Millis she stopped by a local park in Boston with her other son

Michael. My son Austin and Michael started playing and Holly and I started talking. We learned we shared much in common. Our birthdays are exactly one day apart, mine is July 11, 1965, and hers is July 10, 1965. We both are Italian and we both have an autistic child. I gave her my phone number. We've been friends ever since.

Chapter 2 – Life As A Patient

I had been unhappy in my therapy with Dr. Guild so after six months I left. I did it the cowardly way. I called her and left a message on her answering machine telling her I was quitting therapy. She never called me back. That really bothered me that she didn't follow through or ask for a last session. I felt abandoned even though I was the one who had left. It didn't work out because I think I had a deep distain for woman after being emotionally/verbally and physically abused by my mother. Also I believe I just wasn't really serious at the time or committed to really doing therapy.

At the time I left Dr. Guild I was seeing Dr. Alan for free with my husband doing marriage counseling. He was good friends with our minister Weldon, who set us up with him. I loved Alan! He was much older, very lanky with medium straight grey hair that swept around his neck and he sported a mustache. He was also very down to earth and like this woodsy, back to nature guy. The very first session Andrew and I sat down he gave us this gargantuan smile that shot up to the sun and back, so bright it filled the room as he said "What do you need; what do you want?" Gotta love a guy who utters those words the first time you meet!

I confess I loved Dr. Alan so much that for the first time I really wanted to talk about my problems with a professional. But this was marriage counseling and not individual therapy and both Dr. Alan and my husband had to remind me of that. Oh, really! Can't we just kick Andrew out and do one on one? Dr. Alan would get upset at me monopolizing the conversation and even answering the questions that he directed at Andrew. One time he turned to me, pointed his finger and said "You shut up". Yeah I know it's hard to shut me up when I get going. Gotta love a man with balls!

Not only did Dr. Alan have balls but he had brass. He was the first and only therapist to give me an ultimatum. He told me that I needed individual therapy so as not to monopolize the time in the couple's session and also to work on my own issues. If I didn't get that help he refused to do the marriage counseling. It was quite a blow! I couldn't lose Dr. Alan!

This is how I got hooked up with Dr. Eugene Burns. I had not liked my experience with Dr. Guild so I asked Dr. Alan for help in finding a therapist. I wanted an older male. My dad had just died and I was looking for a father figure. So Dr. Alan referred me to Dr. Burns. The first appointment with this very elderly, white haired fat psychologist was terrible. He was flat in personality. He couldn't budge a smile for free and he showed no emotion. I walked in and told him about Dr. Alan saying "I don't want to be here but my marriage counselor gave me an ultimatum that if I didn't find my own psychologist I couldn't continue therapy with him". Well that went over big with him. His ego was bleeding so hard that his chair was turning red. Actually, his chair was already red but I swear it got even more red, or maybe it was his very wrinkled face?

Each session was worse than the last with him. He was narcissistic and lacked empathy and was even cruel. One session he said to me "I can treat you like shit and you'd still come back." I was appalled. I made this man feel so inadequate as a therapist that he took it out on me. He would tell me "You make me feel impotent". I had had it with him and his abuse. So again, after just six months I quit therapy.

This time I did it in an email. And I also made a formal complaint with the licensing board about his behavior, but nothing ever became of that. I will give Dr. Burns credit though, unlike Dr. Guild he DID call and ask me to come in for a session to talk about my wanting to leave. I never did though.

I knew I had to find someone else real soon if I wanted to continue with Dr. Alan. I told Dr. Alan that Dr. Burns was an asshole so I quit him. All growing up I heard about my dad's psychiatrist Dr. Robert Day. The name stuck in my head. I was missing my dad and the combination of wanting to feel closer to my dad by seeking his therapist and also the curiosity of putting a face with that name I heard all the time growing up made me call him. So I called Dr. Day and said do you remember a patient of yours named Anthony Palladino? He said he did. I said "I'm his daughter; can I come in for an appointment." He said sure and so we booked it and onto shrink #3!

This time his office was located in his house. This was a new experience for me. Also he was my first and last psychiatrist. I was a little antsy about seeing a psychiatrist and especially this one because he was my fathers. I walked up this long stairway into this tiny two by four hall between the bathroom and his office. He had no waiting room! In the hall was a tiny chair and some magazines. His office was what must have been an attic bedroom for a guest. The bathroom was rather large with a full bath and shower and the window was open slightly but nailed into place so it could not be opened any more than it was which was about two inches. I suppose he didn't want anyone jumping out of it!

He came out to greet me very coolly, very stern like and quite professionally. He seemed to me more like a medical doctor (which he actually was), but not one you do therapy with. I sat in a high back winged chair and he sat at his desk. He had a very soft voice, looked very astute and was wearing glasses, with his notepad and pen in his lap. He was well fit, in his sixties with some greying hair, but quite handsome. He reminded me of some Hollywood actor from the fifties, but I couldn't tell you who. I told him my dad (his former patient) died. He said he was sorry and spoke very fondly of him. I asked him questions about my dad and he had no trouble answering them.

When I went back and told Dr. Alan this he wasn't too thrilled. He didn't think I should be seeing my father's therapist. He thought there might be a conflict of interest there. But since I did fulfill my obligation to his ultimatum he really couldn't say much. I wasn't too happy with Dr. Day though. I just felt very uncomfortable with him. He felt too contrived and mechanical to me. It did not appear like a good fit and after two failed therapies I did not feel like putting in another six months with this one. So I started looking this time after only two months for another therapist.

This is when I discovered "Psychology Today" website. I highly recommend this website for both psychologists and patients. It gives intensive profiles of each therapist, and everything you need to know about them, including insurance information. Most include a picture of the therapist as well. This is where I stumbled upon the psychologist that would change my life forever. It was fated to happen. And it was the start, the beginning of "coming into myself" for the first time in my life.

I didn't want to end the therapy with Dr. Day until I was sure I had found another psychologist. So I called this new psychologist and made an appointment first with him before seeing Dr. Day the next day. It was April 4, 2005. I had just moved into my new house, a ranch on a quiet dead end street just two months before after selling my parents two family house after they died. This was a day I shall never forget. This was a psychologist that to this day I am still with, whom I still deeply love and who has helped me immeasurably through-out the years. Dr. Love taught me about love, unconditional love.

I walked into Dr. Love's office which was in his home like Dr. Days. But this psychologist had a nice waiting room, with a long wooden table loaded up with more magazines than a newsstand. I already knew some things about him and what he looked like from reading his profile off of "Psychology Today", but nothing could quite prepare me for the face to face experience I had when he opened the door. How many of you remember the scarecrow from the Wizard of Oz? That to me is Dr. Love in looks, and in manner. He came out with the warmest, sincerest smile I had ever seen. He shook my hand and greeted me like I was a guest staying overnight in his home, as if he was honored to have me.

I sat down on his couch and it was so easy to be with him, like we were old friends. The conversation flowed quite naturally. He wasn't shrink like at all! Was this a psychologist? I felt right at home with him.

His office was huge with two couches, a chair, a children's play area with every kind of toy imaginable. He had a desk (other than his own) where patients could draw, paint or write. He was also a child psychologist. We talked, but I didn't feel pressured. I told him I was seeing my father's psychiatrist but that I was unhappy with him. I left making an appointment for the following Monday with Dr. Love. This was it. This was the man. This was the one!

The next day I went in for my last appointment with Dr. Day. No goodbyes through the phone or emails. This time I was going to do it the right way! I told him that I found somebody else. He was shocked. He had no idea I was unhappy. I told him he lacked warmth and was just too robot-like and mechanical. It didn't end bad though. I just think he felt sad. On the other hand I couldn't have been happier than if I won the lottery.

Chapter 3 –The Goodbye Girl

On Psychology Today's website you can write the psychologist and get a response before you even meet them. I wrote Dr. Love my very first email there titled "Looking For Mr. Goodshrink" thinking and referring to the movie "Looking For Mr. Goodbar". Here is his email back to me:

Sent: Monday, March 28, 2005 10:34 PM

Subject: Looking for Mr. Goodshrink

Dear Sandy,

Thanks for your email. As you certainly are aware after all the difficulties with finding the right therapist, what makes most therapies work is finding the right match. It is only when both therapist and patient feel there is a good fit with each other that your sense of self can be rekindled and strengthened. Not so different than your lovely metaphor of the nanny and the child-- although it's not just the child, the nanny contributes also. Not knowing more about your situation, it's difficult to give you advice on how to proceed from here. But if you want to call me, we can talk on the phone about it, or if it seems appropriate after we talk and you're in the Boston area, we can meet to discuss further.

I walked into the second session as if lightning struck me. It had!! I know people talk about love at first sight. Well this was love at second sight. I was mesmerized! This session ran almost two hours!!! It was so intense. I told him I was a damsel in distress and that I was worried about his "rescue hero fantasies". He told me (as others after him had) that I was quite insightful. We discussed about my coming more than once a week. He was a psychoanalysis and that required a commitment of many hours a week of therapy. I told him my insurance would never pay for it. He said "Don't worry about the money". He was going to do it for free! Five hours a week! Mondays were 10:15 – 11:30. Tuesdays were 4:00 -5:30 and

Magical Thursdays (I'll explain later) were
4:00 -6:30.

I started really worrying. I was getting too
close to him. He told me that he went away
for the whole month of August but not to
worry because he would call me every week
and I could come by and visit him at his
vacation home if I needed to! He even gave
me the number there! I never heard of this!

During one session as I was lying down on
his analysis couch he put a blanket over me
and tucked me in. It felt like I was
regressing into a child-like state. I told him I
wanted him to read to me. So he got the
child's book "Alexander and the Terrible,
Horrible, No Good, Very Bad Day" and read
that to me while I was ensconced in his
blanket.

I have never felt love so deeply and
profoundly. I was so scared of this new
feeling. I was terrified of being hurt and
being abandoned. I always tried to run away
and quit therapy. As a result he would chase

me until I would come back. I remember one time trying to quit in July. He wrote me an email telling me his father suffered a severe stroke. My heart just melted and I immediately called him saying "I'm so sorry about your father. Is there anything I can do" He told me "Come back to therapy". His father never did recover from that stroke.

During one session I was having a particularly hard time he came over and sat next to me on the couch and put his arm around my back and held my shoulder with his hand. As he was doing this he asked "Is this alright? I'm crossing a boundary." I told him it was fine. He was so close that I could see each line in his face, as a deep crevice , one filled with the baptismal waters of Jesus. This was a rebirth, an awakening!

As his August vacation was drawing near I was getting more psychotic worrying about how I would handle his absence. I started looking for another psychologist and I found Dr. Michael Steinburg to see me while he was away. They talked on the phone briefly. The last session before his vacation was painful. He held me tightly in his arms before he left for what seemed like an eternity.

   I went to see Dr. Michael Steinburg when Dr. Love was away. He also had an office out of his home. The month I saw Michael all I did was talk about Dr. Love and our relationship. Though Michael was a very nice man he didn't help much. He is an email Dr. Love sent to me while on his vacation about Michael:

Dear Sandy,

   I do understand your worry about getting hurt. You
can't get into a deep or successful therapy without
that worry coming strongly to the surface, and we need
to discuss it. That we can and will do, and you will

discover that the insecurity about getting hurt will
begin to disappear just as the anxiety did. This
therapy is going well and there are lots of
indications that it is helping you and will continue
to help you. As far as the abuse being connected to
your open relationship with your father, that is pure
bull shit. There are obvious issues involved with your
father and the impact of his schizophrenia on you, but
as far as the open relationship you had with him, it
probably saved you from further unbearable suffering.
For someone to tell you otherwise after seeing you for
a couple of sessions is nothing more than shooting
from the hip--and dead wrong.

I am not thinking I am too open with you
and have no
intention of changing my style of work with
you,
Steinburg notwithstanding. In fact, I feel
quite
confident that is what you need. I agree that
it is
the aura and the deep connection that
worries you
rather than anything specific. How can you
not be
worried when this is, as you've said,
probably the
deepest relationship you've allowed yourself
to experience.

You've let yourself take a major risk.
You're going to have to trust me that we can
and will
talk about it and it will help you get better.
As you know, I have a lot of patience and a
strong
belief in you and your being able to use this

intensive therapy well. What I don't have much
tolerance for is some therapist who doesn't know you
very well inappropriately getting in the middle of
your treatment. It is both unfair to you, undermining,
and unhelpful. The job of someone covering in August
is to help get you through the month. If Steinburg
doesn't like your treatment with me, he has only two
ethical choices--tell you to talk it over with me or
tell you to get a consultation. Anything beyond that
verges on the unethical--as does telling you that I am
"stringing you along." If I didn't think therapy with
me was helping you, I would have told you so directly.

There would be no reason not to. But far from it, I
feel just the opposite.
 So there you have some initial, direct reactions.
Hope they at least clarify where I'm coming from. We
will continue onward and work out whatever comes
up, and I will continue to do what we (you and I) think
is helpful for you, regardless of other opinions. I
look forward to talking with you next week and to
seeing you in September.

All I remember Michael saying that whole month to me about my relationship with Dr. Love is "This is confusing". It really doesn't help a patient if the therapist is confused!!

When he came back from his vacation we grew extremely close and the relationship became quite intimate. This was especially true on Thursdays when the sessions were two and a half hours in duration. We coined these sessions "Magical Thursdays". I was totally free for the first time in my life. I use to come to therapy dressed up in all kinds of costumes. I really got to show off my creative side. One time I was dressed as a hooker, with a long blonde wig and short shorts with high heeled boots and a very revealing top. Another time I was Dorothy from the "Wizard Of Oz". I identified strongly with that character because I was always "looking for home". I even bought Dr. Love a Dorothy and Scarecrow Barbie doll for his play area.

Dr. Love and I would lie on the floor together those days and just reflect. Sometimes we didn't even talk. When you are that close you don't need words. They can be just distractions. The therapy was different than any I have ever heard of. I was in a very unique place with this man. He would open up to me about his personal life. And I even got to go inside his home. The first time was around Christmas. I had always grown up with artificial trees that looked so tacky. He would always pick out a real tree with his family. So I asked if I could see it. It was so magical, him and I standing by his tree on a cold winter day. Looking with wonder and awe at both the tree and him. I'll never forget there was a brass star and a moon on the top of the tree revolving around each other.

During this time Dr. Love told me that he loved me. I would often sit in his lap and I felt like I was his and he was mine. But these feelings became over the top for me. I had never in my life experienced these feelings before. This was my first time and I didn't know how to regulate myself. I started running away every couple of weeks from therapy, and I also started losing a lot of sleep. I also was developing an intense jealousy of a very young female patient that came after me on Thursdays. She was pretty with long dark hair and she had her whole life in front of her, while I was a middle-aged unhappily married woman with a severe sick brain-damaged son who didn't know what I wanted out of life. I was also deeply afraid of losing him.

I wrote him yet another goodbye email comparing his young patient to my mother's best friend's daughter, who was my age. My mother was exceptional close to this girl. Her name was Rebecca and I was insanely jealous of her relationship with my mother.

The psychotic goodbye email:

I want out of this therapy. Every article I've read has stated that shrinks save their favorite patients for last so there won't be any interruptions. The 5:40 is your last patient of the day - You never have to rush her out for anyone - yet you had to rush me out for her. It reminds me of all the COUNTLESS talks my mother had with Becca but she would never listen to me.

Remember the saying: Save the BEST for last. I was tormented and picked on mercilessly at school and I would never eat lunch, yet I didn't turn to drugs or fucking every boy in town like Becca, yet she always would LISTEN to her!!! MY OWN FATHER DISCLAIMED me as his REAL daughter - saying my mother fucked my cousin!!!Anyway I can't take it anymore - I've been sick all week. If you call I will IGNORE the phone. I can't do it - I can't come to your house knowing about her being there 4 times a week and the last patient of the day and how I was ousted out when SHE was LATE and dismissed on the phone because of her. I NEVER WILL BE HURT AGAIN!!!

The borderline personality was starting to really come out in this therapy unlike it ever had before. At times I didn't even know who I was anymore. I was starting to hate myself. I kept looking for other therapists as well. I couldn't tolerate the closeness with Dr. Love and all the intense feelings it stirred up in me such as jealousy, insecurity, worthlessness, fear and finally abandonment.

Here is Dr. Love's response email:

Sandy,

You want out? You can't have "out!" I am not willing to disclaim you. You are the most all or nothing patient I have seen in my 30 odd years of doing therapy. But you happen to be the most insightful and loveable one also. The combination, as this crucial issue of specialness emerges, is making you "psychotic"--so you are hereby committed-- to be here at your regular times. If I thought you were going to break your promise, I never would have agreed to your skipping

Monday in the first place. Your running away behavior is such that you don't deserve a day off, so just be here tomorrow where you can be listened to. (And stop reading traditional Internet shrink articles; my least favorite hour of the day to see patients is the last one!)

This would become a frequent occurrence these psychotic emails, along with phone calls all the time, sometimes waking him up in the wee hours of the morning. He would always maintain his empathy and patience with me, at the height of "my attacks" on him. He seemed too good to be real. And even during all this we kept getting closer and closer. One time after we got in a fight he suggested we play the game "Sorry" during a session because he said we were both sorry and didn't handle things well. So there we were on the floor playing Sorry. He was so cute. He would keep his finger on the piece for what seemed like eternity until he decided where to move.

I would still get to be as creative as possible during the sessions. One time I came in with my suitcase telling him "I'm moving in". Actually I had balloons in there with all my different feelings written on them. I would float them high in the air and watch them drift across his office, wishing some of these intense feelings could do just that.........drift away!

Chapter 4 - The Biopsy

It was February of 2006 and I was scheduled for my first mammogram. I was extremely nervous. I had also waited an extra year to get it. So instead of age forty, like the guide-lines recommend I waited until forty-one. I went to Newton-Wellesley Hospital where my sons were both born and my primary doctor's office was. It was quite uncomfortable. I never realized how much they squeeze your breasts. They squeezed so hard that milk was coming out! I had given up breast feeding seven years ago! Now I truly have compassion for cows when they suck out the milk with those machines.

I left the hospital after the mammogram. I didn't think I needed to wait around. Two days later my phone rings. It was the radiology department calling to tell me they saw something on the mammogram and that I needed to come in for further tests. I was hysterical! It was my very first mammogram! Of course I called Dr. Love and he told me I could see him even though I wasn't scheduled. He also tried to soothe me, telling me that it was probably nothing.

I went in for more testing and they found a cluster of cells grouped together and they said they wanted to biopsy it and that I had a 20% chance of cancer. I was totally shaken down. I went into my Thursday session totally beside myself. I talked about everything under the sun EXCEPT my biopsy! I discussed Dr. Love's family and the excitement around the fact that his first grandchild was to be born in June. When I left I felt really upset and again wrote Dr. Love another psychotic email. He wrote me and called me up that Saturday before my biopsy was scheduled on Monday. He told me that he wanted to see me on Sunday before my biopsy. He also wanted to see me the Monday morning immediately following my biopsy.

So I went in that Sunday and Dr. Love was dressed in jeans and sneakers. It was the first time I saw him in casual clothes. He sang to me as I sat on the floor the James Taylor's song "You've Got A Friend". I felt so cared for and loved. It was a Sunday after all and I was taking time away from him being with his family. He held me before I left and wished me luck.

The next day, Monday I went in for the biopsy. I was awake and they used a very large needle to extract the cells to test. I was very sore afterwards and they told me to keep ice on the area. When I got to his home office right away he went in his kitchen and made an ice-pack for me to apply to my breast while I was there. Now it was just the waiting for the results, the most difficult part, to see if it was benign or malignant. I was terrified. It was going to take days to find out!

I wanted to run away again. It seems like this kept happening. Dr. Love said I was like the "Runaway Bunny" in the children's story by that name. He wrote me a very touching email:

Dear Runaway Bunny,

While you are out in the woods terrified and alone and fragmenting, you might want to consider the following thoughts:

1) Runaway bunnies don't want to be lost, they want to be found; that's why they run away. There should be a banner above your hutch to remind you of that: Find Me.

2) Those that care deeply for a runaway bunny WANT to accompany them through good times and awful times. They do not get frightened off or worn down by need. Another sign to put above your hutch: Connectedness Works.

3) Those that care deeply about a runaway bunny feel hurt when they are not allowed to express that caring. Guilt be damned.

So I expect this runaway bunny to show up at the one place she won't feel alone at 4.

Chief Rabbit

I went into the next session feeling sore and sporting a huge bruise on my left breast where they did the biopsy. I undid my blouse and bra and showed the bruise to Dr. Love. He didn't act put off or uncomfortable about me doing this. We were so close that it just felt natural to want to show him the site where they did the biopsy. I also gave him a stuffed rabbit that he still has in his office to this day. Around the rabbits' neck I hung a sign that said "Chief Rabbit". That is how Dr. Love signed his "Runaway Bunny" email. To this day not only does he still have the rabbit but the sign is also still there well in tact!

A couple of months had gone by and it was now April of 2006. It was a whole year in therapy with Dr. Love!! ONE YEAR! I had

never lasted that long with anyone else. So I
bought a card for the occasion and I had
baked a chocolate cupcake and brought in a
big candle of the number for the top. We sat
together on the couch, which we had been
doing lately. When we   were this close I
often stroked his arm. I loved his arms! Oh,
sorry for getting off the subject. He just has
nice arms. He works out. What was I
saying? Oh, right he has nice arms. No
seriously it was our one year anniversary.

Dr. Love excused himself and went in his
house and came back with two cups, a
container of milk and matches. He lit the
candle and poured us organic milk in the
cups (he only does organic). After we both
blew out the candle he split the cupcake I
made into two pieces and we each ate a half.
It was a very special time indeed. It had
been a very special year, one fraught with
anxieties, and fears but most of all love. You
never forget the people who were there for
you. This man did it all for free. He wasn't

getting paid. The care he gave was from his heart.

What I did after this was unforgivable. After all that Dr. Love had given of himself, his time, his care and his love I played a "Judas" on him and betrayed him and all the trust he put in me by going to the licensing board.

Chapter 5 - The Board

It was May of 2006 when I flipped out and mailed a formal complaint to the licensing board. It was a detailed letter of all the very private and personal things Dr. Love shared with me about his personal life. It also included all the touching and unconventional and unorthodox ways that he did therapy. Though I had always loved this man's "out of the box" methods I was upset at him and wanted to punish him. Why? You may ask after all he did for me? I'm a borderline. OK, that is NO excuse. But I didn't know how to love and I was always running away and maybe I wanted to hurt him BFORE he dumped me. This all doesn't make sense now because I think I can tolerate love and being in an intimate relationship.

Hold onto your hats now! This is the very borderline psychotic email I sent him about going to the board:

It's ALL OVER NOW FOR REAL. Yesterday I mailed a formal complaint to the Board with explicit details of everything. Your FATAL error was lying to me.

I have zero tolerance for lies. You're a sweet talker and a charmer and

Will say just about anything. More than feeling loved and special I wanted a REAL relationship - which you simply could not give me because the past year was based on lies.

The borderline personality goes from idealizing to demoralizing. And they also have severe abandonment issues usually from traumatic childhood injuries. They want to be loved but are scared so they push it away. I could write another book on this alone "My Life As A Borderline" What do you think, maybe my next book? Doctors don't like to take on borderlines. You see why? They are extremely high-risk patients. Many are cutters and suicidal and dangerous. Fortunately for me I do NOT fit into that category. Now the "plain nuts" one I do fit in!

Here is Dr. Love's very loving email back about my going to the board:

Sandy,

So you've done something to try to finalize the pushing me away. I know you're in a rage, and I think there are many things you're feeling rageful about--my vacation, my having gone to Nebraska, the patient that reminded you of your father, my not working on Memorial Day--I could go on, although I'm not sure what you mean by my lying to you. I also think your rage helps to keep you more together when you are feeling "ready to snap." All of this can be dealt with, if you're willing to come in and talk about it, by getting underneath the rage instead of staying in the middle of it. I also think we need to talk about your disappointment in this relationship not being as real as you want. I still want/expect to see you Monday.

49

I felt so guilty after I mailed that off. I had to do something and right away! It could ruin Dr. Love. So I ran down to the licensing board office in Boston and told them I made a terrible mistake and wanted to rescind the complaint but they couldn't find it!!! I was having a fit. They took down all the information and told me that when they track the letter that they will execute it. Whew!! I just got by on my skin teeth with that one! I called Dr. Love and told him and he told me to come in for my session, which was not easy.

I could tell when I went in for my next session that there was some repairing to do. Dr. Love said "You crossed a line". Yup, I sure did. I asked him how he felt. He was quite bold. He said "Part of me wanted to tell you to get the fuck out and leave". I asked him why he didn't do just that and he said "because there is a real relationship here." So what is the lesson? Love forgives. It is hard to believe but we got even deeper and closer after this!

It was now June of 2006. Dr. Love's first granddaughter was born. It was a Saturday and I was out. When I got back home there was this message on my answering machine from Dr. Love telling me that the baby had finally arrived! I was so excited for him! I immediately called and ordered a big basket of flowers and a teddy bear to his house. It arrived the same day. I felt so part of his life and family even though I wasn't directly involved with them.

We were getting even closer, if that's possible (given how close we were). I remember one session I went in dressed in a bikini toting a huge branch of part of an oak tree that had fallen in my back yard after a storm. I pretended that branch was a palm tree and that I was going on a tropical vacation. After all I was wearing my bikini. One time he brought me into his workshop and showed me all his tools. He hand-crafted everything in his office from his own desk to the clock on his wall.

Of course my borderline self-started to sexualizes everything and when I was in his lap I grabbed his penis. Let me put this straight he never touched me sexually. Yes, he allowed touch but non-sexual touch. I was always trying to sexualize the relationship and one time I completely stripped naked for him.....but that's later on. So you need to keep reading.

It was starting to get close to his vacation again. This time I told him I had a bad feeling about it. I didn't quite know why but I had a gut feeling that bad things were going to happen. He thought it was just my usual anxiety about his going away. But no, this felt very different. Sometimes people of a premonition about things before they happen. I don't often get them, but this time I did. And I was right. The summer of 2006 was going to be a real bad one that first started out with a head-on car crash and ended up with my son needing heart surgery.

Chapter 6 – Austin's Heart Surgery

The first day of Dr. Love's vacation my husband along with my son got in a head-on collision. Luckily no one was hurt but the car was wrecked. A teen-age girl reversed direction completely on the high-way and plowed head-on into us. We all got out of it unscathed. The girl was badly shaken though, because it was her parents car. But ironically her car had no damage. We were stranded out in the middle of the highway. The tow-truck that took our car said he could only take one of us and my husband didn't want to leave my son and I alone out in the middle of heavy traffic. So after the teen-age girl that was responsible for the accident talked to the police she drove us home. After all, her car was fine and it was the least she could do. She had all these sexy bras and panties strewn all over the backseat and she kept telling us she was a model. I wonder what kind!

I got home and immediately called Dr. Love and we talked, even though it was his first day on vacation. I started getting the feeling this was going to be a bad summer. I had no idea how right actually right I was! Because shortly after this Austin having severe heart problems. I already had one permanently sick child the thought of having another one was completely daunting!

! It was a summer afternoon and Austin and I were planning on going to the MDC pool to cool off, when Austin told me he didn't feel good. He felt hot but when I looked at him his chest was heaving right out of his shirt! I put my hand on his chest and I swear I could feel his heart as if it was pulsating right there in my hand. I rushed him to the E.R. and the doctors were shocked that he was even standing!!!! He had severe tachycardia and the doctors needed to bring it way down and fast because a heart rate like that was quite dangerous. He could go into cardiac arrest and die! The hooked him up and had the paddles to stimulate his heart if it should stop ready This was extremely frightening!!!! Alex had lost his mind and now it looked like I was going to lose Austin to a severe heart problem.

After this "ordeal" Austin had to see a cardiologist. Dr. Becker had to hook Austin up to a heart monitor that he needed to wear 24/7 - all day and all night for weeks! She told him what to do if he got the tachycardia again. Austin started sinking into a depression. He was so worried to do anything that was the least bit strenuous, that his poor heart wouldn't be able to take it. I was so upset and of course I turned to Dr. Love on his vacation again!

Dr. Love was right there for me as always and offered to pay my way to come see him at his summer home which was several states away. I could take a train there. I wanted to but I felt like this would be taking advantage of him so I thanked him but politely declined. We just stayed in touched through the phone and emails the rest of the summer. I asked Dr. Love when he came back in the fall if he could see Austin himself for therapy because Austin was really depressed about his heart condition.; Of course Dr. love readily agreed to see him.

It turned out that Austin had a faulty wire in his heart. The doctors said he had two options, either go on heart medication for the rest of his life or have heart surgery which carried some risks. As a mother I believe in allowing my son to make his own life choices, including his own mistakes, even at the tender young age of eight. I have never regretted doing that to this day because Austin is a level-headed independent sixteen year old that wants to go to college and take up robotic engineering. He wants to own his home too!

So we let Austin decide and he decided on having the surgery done instead of being on drugs the rest of his life. I told Dr. Love about this and he said he wanted to come to the hospital while Austin was in surgery to offer me moral support. The only other person who came to the hospital other than Dr. Love and my husband was my good friend Lorrie, who was the leader of a jazz band. I have known her since Austin was in a stroller. She is like a mother figure to me. She also visited Austin the afternoon before his surgery and bought him a humungous stuffed bear which he brought with him to the hospital.

My husband and I stayed by Austin's side the who time, even staying overnight in his room. He was grueling to say the least. But when you hear the doctor come out of surgery and say "We got it!" the hell we went through was all worth it! The surgery was a success! They got the faulty wire and Austin never had a problem again with his heart!

Chapter 7 – The Stripper

It's my claim to fame! Dr. love wrote papers and gave speeches across the country about this one! It's the day I stripped and offered Dr. Love a blowjob! I was in love with Dr. Love. I never felt this way before about anyone. So during one session, almost two years into the therapy I wanted to finally share everything, including my body with him. We had been through so much together and I have never gotten that deep with anyone. I was starting to feel sexually aroused. I don't know how and I can't explain it because we were not sitting together or touching one another. In fact, during this session we were a good distance apart.

I was feeling aroused and I said "I'm feeling wet". My panties were so soaked it's as if I pissed in them! Then I took off my shirt and bra. He didn't tell me to stop. He just kept watching, so I continued and took off my pants and very wet panties. I brought the wet panties over to him and wiped them on his bare arm saying "This is how wet you get me". I also said "I want to suck your cock". I once sent him a rather lengthy email describing in detail how I would actually give him a blowjob, play by play, including licking his balls and taking them in my mouth.

As I told him how much I wanted to suck his cock my hands made their way to his pants to unzip his zipper to get at his penis. But before I could even reach his pants he grabbed my wrists tightly and firmly and stopped me. So here I was completely naked on bended knee ready to give him the blowjob of his life, and here he was holding my wrists tightly. I don't remember exactly what he said but he sure as hell wasn't going to allow me to give him that scrumptious blowjob, that I so wanted to do. After realizing this I told him I would get dressed. He trusted me enough to let go of my wrists. And I did just that. I got dressed, putting everything back on, except I couldn't find my bra!! Dr. Love spotted it, picked it up and tossed it to me! So I can honestly say Dr. Love's hands were in my bra.....only I wasn't wearing the bra at the time!

When I finished getting dressed I left. It was the end of the session. I went home and wrote Dr. Love a very tender email about how well he handled that session. I cannot locate that email; otherwise I would include it here. But I need to say that Dr. Love made me feel accepted as a real person. He did not turn away from me when I took my clothes off but he didn't take advantage of me by allowing me to give him a blowjob.

If Dr. Love had tried to stop me from taking my clothes off or turned away from me in any manner I would have felt severely rejected. If Dr. Love had allowed me to actually give him the blowjob I would have probably felt used and that would make him unethical by getting sexually getting involved with a current patient. We never did discuss the stripping at that time. I later brought it up many years later when I asked him if he ever wrote about it and he told me he had. I have the article he wrote on my stripping. It is far too long to include here...just mail me a self-addressed stamped envelope and include $20.00 and I will rush it off to you!

I started having these sexual "spanking fantasies" about Dr. Love. Now I've never been into S&M, nor has any man physically abused me. I wouldn't want any man to either. And my father not only ever laid a hand on me but he never even dared to raise his voice to me, even when I was being impossible. I started seeing Dr. Love as the stern father type, even though he was really mild mannered. Many patients compared him to Mr. Rogers from the children's television show "Mr. Roger's Neighborhood".

Dr. Love was old enough to be my father. He was over two decades older than me. The spanking fantasies were of me naked in his lap spanking me while his pants were undone and I was sucking his cock. I had to fit a blowjob in there somewhere. Did I mention I like performing blowjobs? I shared my fantasy with him, as many patients do. It is perfectly normal to have sexual fantasies about one's psychologist. But it is not normal to try to act them out.

One time I did try to act out the spanking fantasy. While I was sitting on the floor with Dr. Love I climbed into his lap. Then I spread myself across him with my ass sticking out into the air. I was fully dressed though. I figured if I tried to pull my pants down he would remove me off his lap. Then I took his loose, limp hand and started delivering blows with it to my buttock. I cried out "your spanking me" but he retorted "you're making me do that" Guess you could say it was a half-ass fantasy come true.

Chapter 8 – Burnout

I write this with a heavy heart. It was the spring of 2007 when I noticed changes in Dr. Love. When one is emotionally and physically intimate with someone they can be acutely aware of any slight change that other people wouldn't necessarily even know existed. None of Dr. Loves other patients were even aware of his burnout. He later told me I was the only one.

Psychologists work long hours and often deal with many high maintenance patients. It's not exactly a nine to five job. Many take phone calls on evenings and weekends and have to be present when a patient is hospitalized, even on their off time. I profoundly admire and respect this profession. Dr. Love was one of these rare psychologists who went above and beyond what most are willing to do. His cell phone was on 24/7 for patients to reach him, nights, weekends, holidays and even his vacation. He never "shut off", almost super human. As a result of this he burned out.

He always called several times during April vacation week. That is when he was away across the country visiting his in-laws. This April vacation was quite different. He called only once and it was an exceptionally brief conversation with him abruptly ending it in a matter of minutes. I was crushed. The emails stopped coming as well. When I would wrote him he didn't write back. I was devastated. I didn't know what was happening or what I did wrong. When I brought this up to him he said that nothing had changed and he felt exactly the same way about me.

To prove to myself that he still loved me I asked to see him one Saturday after he got back from his long flight from his in-laws. He reluctantly agreed to it. I told him I wanted to go to the park with him. It was a warm, sunny spring day in April. He said that I didn't "really need" to see him but I pleaded and he relented. I never use to have to plead to see him before and I felt deeply crushed. But I convinced myself that he must still love me because he was willing to see me on a Saturday just for fun, knowing I was ok and not of any need for psychological help.

I drove to his house with the windows cranked all the way down to catch the warm breeze, and had the radio blaring loud. I was happy as a lark! I was seeing the man I loved and going to the park. I brought my son's football for us to toss around. When I arrived I sat crisscrossed on his neighbor's tree stump and waited for him to come out of his house. I didn't want to ring his door and disturb his family. He came out unshaven, unkempt, wearing sunglasses and black jeans and sneakers. He was sporting this Cheshire cat smile as if he was very happy to see me.

We proceeded to walk to a near-by park in his neighborhood. When we got there we tossed the football around. It was a busy day at the park. There was baseball game going on nearby and children were playing on the swings and playground equipment. After we got done playing catch we laid on the grass. He laid completely down with is elbows stretched out and hands entwined behind his head. I started swirling a blade of the fresh green grass of early spring. I went to touch him and he said "not here". Of course people knew him there. He was on his own turf. We just stayed like that, no words. It was the last good memory that I have of him. Tears are welling in my eyes as I write this.

I love you Dr. Love. I will never forget all that you gave of yourself. I will always hold onto my treasure box of the very special moments we shared. You truly were one of a kind. You gave and you gave until there was no more left of you to give. Ironically years later he told me he felt like "The Giving

Tree" a children's book by Shel Silverstein. It's a must read for adults as well as for children. It's about a boy who keeps taking and taking from a tree. First he uses its branches to hold a swing. Then he eats of the trees apples and later he cuts down the trees wood to build a boat and then a house until all that is left of the tree is a stump. By this time the boy is an old man and all that he needs of the tree is a stump to rest on. The problem with me is that Dr. Love had become a stump but I never grew up into the old man who was quite content with it. I was still the impetuous boy who took the tree for granted.

This time when Dr. Love was on his summer vacation in the summer of 2007 there were no phone calls at all to me and very few emails. I was truly on my own. My heart was broken. I decided I needed to do something for myself so I decided to find a job. I got a job at the local mall as a security officer. This would cut into my hours with Dr. Love. The relationship was already declining anyway. He wouldn't allow me to touch him anymore, so I was cut off both emotionally and physically. The job was the only thing that truly saved me from further heartache.

When Dr. Love came back in the fall I told him about my new job. I told him that I would have to cut many hours out of the therapy because of it. He told me, the very first session back, that he too would have to cut back as well my time to drive his daughter to basketball practice. Again I was devastated. My new job was taking enough hours away and now this news that he was going to take even more hours away was just too much to endure. And along with the growing chasm between, us I saw no point in continuing the therapy with him anymore.

I stormed out of that session and left this time for good.....almost. I left for a long while, many months. It was the first time my "goodbye" really stuck. He didn't chase me this time either. Everything was different; everything had changed. I had to let go of him and focus on my job. There I met another man I was very much attracted to. His name was Gary Mavis and he was the manager of Simmons jewelry store at the mall. We developed this wild and passionate attraction. I would sneak into back hallways in the malls (where the customers are not allowed) just to kiss him. Ironically at the same time my husband was working at Border's Bookstore at that very same mall! So all this was happening right under my husband's nose!

Gary was handsome as hell, but tiny, jockey style, with jet black hair. For a small guy you could feel his presence fiercely. He dominated a room when he walked into it. I was drawn to his fierce and dominating presence but I was also put off by his arrogance and lack of warmth. So although I was quite hot for him I declined all his attempts of asking me out on a date. It was just as well. He moved to the mall in New York. And I don't do long distance relationships.

Chapter 9 – Board AGAIN!

After I left Dr. Love I still kept in contact with him through email. And after a few months I decided to come back but it was hard for him to find me a slot. He was a very popular psychologist and no sooner than I left my old slots were quickly filled. Eventually he found me a time on Thursdays in January of 2008. It was only an hour though, unlike our "magical Thursdays" of yesteryear that went two and a half hours. I asked him why he couldn't extend it and he said because he had to drive his daughter to basketball practice, (as he told me in September right before I quit).

I started resuming the therapy after many months away, but it felt estranged, artificial and contrived. He wasn't the same and the old relationship was gone. It was very hard to do therapy under these conditions. Then after one session I noticed a patient waiting for him after I came out. I thought he said that he couldn't extend my session because he had to drive his daughter. I was livid at him! It appeared he had lied to me.

I called him quite upset and told him I saw a man go in after me when I thought he had to drive his daughter. He explained on the phone that he didn't have to drive his daughter "every week". Well if that was so, I asked him why he wouldn't choose to see me then, extend my session (like the old days) and he told me because sometimes he's just too tired to work. I was fuming at him and felt completely abandoned. I told him I was going to the board and reporting him. I also felt deeply upset because he had previously told me his wife drove his daughter one day to basketball practice and he did it another day (which was my time on Thursdays). I knew if he had picked the other day to drive his daughter (the day his wife drove her) he would have had to cut into another patients time (the one I was insanely jealous of). I thought he chose her over me.

It started to seem like everything was unravelling again and this time worse than ever. How could I ever trust him? I didn't know which end was up and I felt betrayed and deeply abandoned. Again, I wrote him

another psychotic email about my going to
the board. This would make it the second
time now. The first time being in May of
2006....this was less than two years later.

Here is my email threatening the board:

I heard you say in September that you had
to cut me short on Thursdays because you
had to drive your daughter. Now you're
telling me you see a patient on some
Thursdays. If you're not seeing them or
driving your daughter "you're too tired to
work". You took away my Thursdays to see
the 5:40 girl, whom is the special one now.
You see her every day. But you lied and said
you were driving your daughter. You knew
since November (I have confirmation) that I
wanted to see you, yet you chose her for that
time over me, when she see you every day!!!!
I've had enough and am going to the board.
You have broken me. I am a broken woman
over you. I want you to realize just how bad
it's been and I'm sure the board will make
you quite aware of your emotional neglect

and abandonment of me. How could it ever come to this?

And here is his response back:

Sandy,

 It can only "come to this" if you do what you say is your life long pattern--that is as soon as you begin to get what you want or establish or re-establish a relationship, you try to destroy it by pushing people away or running away. So you fight to resume therapy and then try to find reasons to end it. I hope you decide to come in on Thursday instead of permanently destroying any possibility of a relationship.

It didn't matter what he said. I went and mailed a formal second complaint to the licensing board. But I also, on the other hand wanted to get a mediator to try to help us both resolve the matter and the extreme hurt. I wasn't out to "get him" I was out to "get it" resolved.

Here is an email to Dr. Love explaining my desperation for help:

I already contacted the board and they will get back to me and want to meet with me, as well as with you. I'm sure by now you have angry and hurt feelings as well as I do. I think we CAN work it out but it's gone too far for us to do alone. Think about when couples come to you for a last ditch effort to save their marriage, why? because they simply can't do it alone. I feel very strongly this is the case with us. I am asking (BEFORE I go to the board with this request) if we can get a mediator as an impartial person to help us facilitate our feelings with each other. I would much rather do this than go in there and vent my anger and hurt and you go in there and explain your part.

It is my personal opinion that you regressed me as a child and I clung to you and couldn't function without the 100% love/devotion I was used to, the "slightest" change (misstep) and I fell apart. But that's just my take on it. Yes, I betrayed you and divulged personal information, and along with all the running away you might want nothing further to do with me at this point. Usually when a partner betrays it is a cry for help. This is up to you. It's just my personal opinion that we can't do it alone and that we need help.

 I feel strongly that it's worth saving but I also feel very strongly that we need help (a mediator).If I was vengeful and out to hurt you I would never ask for this, and if you agree to it I think it will only help you as well. It's entirely up to you. I'm really sorry for the betrayal, but NOT sorry that I did what I felt needed to be done. So maybe you should give it some thought. I thought long and hard about it and I'm in so much pain and depression over this relationship (or lack of it) that I needed outside help.

 Sandy

Here is Dr. Love's response back:

Sandy,

 I have always been willing to do a consultation with you, and I still am. And as I've told you on the phone, I'm extremely sorry you're in so much pain and depression. As I also told you in a previous email, I wouldn't have found a time for you to come back after you quit if I didn't care about you enormously and think things could be worked out. I still think they can.

Unfortunately, in a vengeful and hurt state, (your "psychotic rage") you've precipitated an adversarial legal situation in which you've pitted the two of us against each other. So from my perspective there are only two choices and you have to decide which you want. You can either withdraw your complaint and we can consult someone to see if we can get back on track in this relationship (and I do agree with you that we can work it out), or you can proceed with your complaint and totally end the relationship.

But, assuming you've gone through with a formal complaint, it is not feasible for me to be attempting to work anything out with you while being put in an adversarial legal position. So really the decision is yours, and I hope you decide to try to work it out. That certainly would be my choice.

Again I withdrew the complaint with the board, but not in person. This time I called them over the phone. And I continued my therapy with Dr. Love but it wouldn't last for long. In less than a year I would be leaving again. I just couldn't recapture the "magic" that we shared, very similar to when people fall out of love.

Chapter 10 – A Very Bad Year

I ended therapy again in the fall of 2008. I
needed another breast biopsy. What
happened in 2006 happened again and the
doctors found a group of cells that looked
suspicious. But this time Dr. Love was
completely insensitive and uncaring. When I
told him how scared I was about it he
replied: "you already were through it
before". I could not believe that this was the
same man that brought me an ice-pack and
sang to me James Taylor's song "You've Got
A Friend" during my first biopsy! After this
complete lack of care I had had it with Dr.
Love.

Luckily, like the first biopsy everything
turned out fine. Even though I left therapy I
still stayed in touch through emails and
phone contact with Dr. Love. One evening
Dr. Love called with some very disturbing
news. This was April of 2009. He told me
that his was diagnosed with breast cancer.
Those are the worse words any woman can
hear! I just broke down completely on the
phone as he said this. I started shaking very

badly and sobbing uncontrollably. I told him that I was so sorry. I couldn't sleep that night and it was very difficult to stop shaking.

As his wife was scheduled for surgery I decided to get her a fruit basket and card letting her know that I was thinking of her. I thought about my own two biopsies and how frightened I was to hear those words. I could really empathize with what she was going through! After the surgery she needed to be on daily radiation treatments as well that would zap her of her energy. She would also need to be on medication for the next five years that had an increase of giving someone uterine cancer. Years later when she had break-through bleeding she was rushed in for an emergency D&C because of the risk of this.

As if his wife's breast cancer wasn't bad enough Dr. Love's father passed away the very next month. He never recovered from his stroke in 2006 and was living in a place for Alzheimer's patients. I bought Dr. Love a big plant in memory of his dad. The month after this Dr. Love went in for shoulder surgery – a rotator cuff tear. It was a very bad year 2009 for him, his wife's cancer, his father's death the next month and then his shoulder surgery the month after that!

That summer of 2009 I started drinking for the very first time – vodka, particularly Smirnoff. And I use to kid around saying I have a new doctor now, Dr. Smirnoff. I would drink and drive. I got drunk so much one time, that I fell down the flight of stairs leading to my basement. As a result I got a sprained ankle. I had to go into work the next day without my foot properly fitting into my shoe and barely being able to walk! I was a security officer and walking was a requirement on the job. In fact, we were not allowed to sit. One of the cleaning ladies that I was friends with helped me along into the rest room where she took a picture of my badly swollen foot and posted it up on Facebook!

I knew I was rapidly going down-hill fast. I didn't have a therapist anymore. I felt completely abandoned by Dr. Love and I knew he had his own problems to deal with, although we did have brief phone contact with one another once a week. I decided it was time to seek a new therapist. And I decided to look once again on Psychology Today's website. After all, that is where I found Dr. Love. It was the worst mistake of my life this time! My husband didn't have a very good job at the book-store and our insurance was even worse. Many therapists would not even take it. I saw Dr. Love for free so I was really spoiled. But I did come across one therapist whose office was practically in my back yard. I could walk to it, and he only charged $25.00 a session!

So I emailed this therapist who was a licensed social worker named William Koot. asking about setting up an appointment. He emailed me right back and we set a date. It was the first time I saw a social worker. I had only gone to psychologists before. A social worker doesn't have to have a PHD in psychology. I had only worked with doctors before. I wasn't sure if the quality of care would be as good. That was an understatement! It was the worse care I had ever received. But I was very desperate and he was very cheap.

You need to really trust your gut instincts. I didn't and it badly burned me. But I was heartbroken over Dr. Love and drinking heavy. I didn't have anyone really to turn to. So I made my way over to the clinic and had my first session with "Bill" the pervert.

Chapter 11 – The Pervert

It was the fall of 2009. I will never look at Rudolph The Red Nose Reindeer again the same way. Remember the chubby snowman in the story? He was played by Burl Ives and Bill reminded me of him. When I first came in the session room at the local clinic he had on this Hawaiian shirt that was much too small for his rather portly stomach. You could see the blubber hanging low when he sat down. I immediately started talking about Dr. Love and our unique and special relationship. He started asking me these far – out questions like which vibrator I used? He knew specifically all the different kinds and variations of vibrators out on the market. I didn't even tell him I masturbated! How could he come up with that kind of question beats me!

I saw this guy for what he was...a creep but still was desperate because of my drinking and lack of insurance. So if I could talk him down to $20.00 for an hour and he would shut up long enough to listen to me pine about Dr. Love we would have ourselves a deal. He agreed to those conditions. And like I said, I could literally walk to his office, it was that close!

But Bill didn't keep his part of the bargain and further kept bringing up sexually inappropriate material during the sessions. When I told him I befriended Jimmy, a middle age man who was brain damaged and was in a wheel chair from the result of a car accident he asked me "did you give him a blowjob?" I told him I was just friends with him. Then Bill said "but didn't you feel sorry for him" and I said "yes, but I don't give blowjobs to people because I feel sorry for them." What an idiot! Then Bill kept asking if I was attractive to him and I emphatically said "NO". He told me a female patient of his once offered to give him a blowjob as payment for the session.

I got fed up with Bill's nonsense and left telling him he is inappropriate during the sessions with sexual talk that has no place in the session and that I was leaving. So I left after a couple of months. But my depression kept growing and I was drinking very heavy and feeling desperate again. So I decided if I could talk the creep down to $15.00 an hour

I would give him a second chance. This was a very bad mistake. I told Bill "no sex talk" and I only pay him $15.00 for the hour. He agreed and sounded glad to have me back.

So now that Bill couldn't talk about sex all he kept doing during the sessions was belittling Dr. Love. He kept saying how Dr. Love only gives me minutes each week on the phone while he on the other hand gives me a whole hour! He also said of Dr. Love's treatment "you walked in his office with five or six problems and walked out with seven or eight", meaning my development of alcohol use and abuse. I admit that was the one thing he said that was dead-on. It was true! I had more problems leaving Dr. Love than I did when starting the therapy!

One night I was so upset over the loss and depth of my relationship with Dr. Love that I called Bill on his cell phone. I was crying to him about Dr. Love and quite vulnerable. First he said "We must talk about this money situation. I can't afford to just take $15.00 anymore; we need to raise it to 20.00." What a time to bring up financial matters about the session when your patient is crying her eyes out over a loss!

The next thing he did was unforgivable. He asked me if I was getting excited on the phone and how close to orgasm I was on a scale of one through ten. He said " How close are you to orgasm right now, an eight I bet". I could not believe what I was hearing! How does one mistake crying for moaning in ecstasy? I hung up the phone fast. I was in total shock and disbelief. I knew this guy was scum and I couldn't believe that I had put up with him this far.

The next day I skipped my session and filed a formal complaint with the licensing board. I did not tell him about the complaint. I never talked to that idiot again! He called of course saying that I owed him money and asked what had happened to me. Then he gave me his home address where I could mail him a $20.00 check.

After I made the complaint a lawyer from the board contacted me and I had to explain everything in detail to her. They investigated the matter. But it takes years for these things to get underway. There was enough "dirt" on Bill to go through a trial and they set a hearing date, which would mean that both He and I would be there with our lawyers and get to tell "our story" and they would make a judgment on it. But it never even got go to trial because the day before Bill officially surrendered his license. SUCCESS, made easy!

Chapter 11 – The Pervert

DEVAL L. PATRICK
GOVERNOR

TIMOTHY P. MURRAY
LIEUTENANT GOVERNOR

GREGORY BIALECKI
SECRETARY OF HOUSING
AND ECONOMIC DEVELOPMENT

COMMONWEALTH OF MASSACHUSETTS
OFFICE OF PROSECUTIONS
Division of Professional Licensure
1000 Washington Street • Boston • Massachusetts • 02118

BARBARA ANTHONY
UNDERSECRETARY OF OFFICE
OF CONSUMER AFFAIRS AND
BUSINESS REGULATION

MARK R. KMETZ
DIRECTOR, DIVISION OF
PROFESSIONAL LICENSURE

Via First Class Mail

June 12, 2012

Sandra Wyllie
35 Hazelmere Road
Roslindale, MA 02131

      RE: In the Matter of William
            Docket No. SW-10-

Dear Ms. Wyllie:

As you are aware, you filed a complaint with the Board of Social Workers against the above referenced individual. The Board investigated the matter and forwarded your complaint to our office.

I write this letter is to inform you that the Board and Mr.   entered into a Consent Agreement. Mr.   agreed to **VOLUNTARILY SURRENDER** his license to practice in resolution of the case. The Board executed the agreement effective June 8, 2012.

If you have any questions regarding this matter, please do not hesitate to contact the Prosecuting Counsel Julie Brady, at (617) 727-**1204**. Your cooperation in this matter is greatly appreciated.

Sincerely,
Amy Riordan
Amy Riordan
Administrative Assistant II

TELEPHONE: (617) 727-1204   FAX: (617) 727-2328   TTY/TDD: (617) 727-2099   http://www.mass.gov/dpl

Chapter 12 – I Came In Fifteen Minutes

In the fall of 2010 I started seeing a new psychologist Dr. Mark Greene but because of the deductible I had at the time I had to pay him $50.00 a session on top of my insurance. I wanted to invest money this time to get a good psychologist, and in my eyes Dr. Greene was a good psychologist. He told me that everything that gets triggered in your present is something that came from your past. I got to understand why I became reactive to certain people and in certain situations. But even though he was helpful, eating up $50.00 a week out of my pocket was becoming a nightmare. We couldn't afford to pay all our bills because of the two hundred dollars extra handed over for therapy a month and in the end I had to drop him.

A funny thing happened though in his waiting room. I was sitting reading a magazine and who should come out of his office but Dr. Burns (my second psychologist with whom I went to the board also). I looked at Dr. Burns and said "hi". He smiled and said "hello". Obviously he didn't recognize me! He was seeing Dr. Greene as a patient too! Many psychologists have their own psychologist, because they are people too, with problems. One day I hope the world will recognize that everyone should see a therapist like they see their primary doctor to maintain good physical health. Good mental health is just as important to maintain. I believe even a well-adjusted person with no outward appearances of anything in particular could use therapy once a month just to "touch base".

During this time as well I implored Dr. Love to give me another chance to do therapy. He offered me fifteen minutes on a Friday, instead of phone contact. FIFTEEN MINUTE THERAPY. This was a grave mistake. I felt so belittled and devalued. No one can do therapy in fifteen minutes. It is far too short. One time his wife called during the session and he ran out just after five minutes because she forgot her license and needed it to board a plane. I was livid! Not only was the relationship dissolved but it was now hurting me more than ever. I wanted to show him how much I was hurting. So one session I came in drunk and told him that I was drinking. And he let me go home that way!

I left therapy yet AGAIN, my third time in the spring of 2011. I came back, as always, a few months later in the summer. It was quite by accident. I was drinking one lonely Saturday night and was feeling rather melancholy and called Dr. Love's number but hung up just before it went to his answering machine. I did not leave a message. Minutes later he called me back and asked if I called. I said "yes I did but I didn't leave you a message" He asked how I was feeling and I said "ok". Then there was a long silence. And I broke down and told him that I missed him and wanted to see him. He told me to come in the following Monday.

When I went to see him that Monday I made it clear there would be no more going back to "fifteen minute sessions". He agreed. So I started seeing him for forty minutes at nine o'clock on Mondays. I have been going strong with that time and day for three years now.

Around the fall of 2011 I also started seeing Dr. Michael Steinburg again as well. I saw Dr. Love on Mondays and Michael on Fridays. I think I felt the need to have more than one therapy session a week. My husband was out of work at this time and things were a strain financially. I was only working part-time as a security officer at The Atrium Mall in Newton but things were starting to shift at work. More and more stores were closing and I was growing unhappy. They moved me across the street to the Mall at Chestnut Hill but I wasn't content there either.

When I told Michael that I was seeing Dr. Love as well he wasn't happy about it. Both psychologists agreed you should only be seeing one therapist at a time or it becomes very confusing for the patient. I strongly disagreed with this narrow minded way of thinking. I explained I have a dentist for my teeth, a primary care for regular check-ups, a GI guy for my digestive tract and so on.... I think they thought that this "didn't wash" because they were both "head guys", you don't have two primary care doctors, or two dentists. But you know what I say to that, and you can quote me on this "Two heads are better than one!" After only a few months I had to stop seeing Michael anyway because of insurance issues. My husband's insurance changed through unemployment and Michael didn't take the new insurance.

Chapter 13 – Multiples

Following the last chapter of "I came in fifteen minutes" this one "Multiples" must have you intrigued! Yes, I have a dirty mind! But no, it's not about multiple orgasms. It's about multiple shrinks.....three to be exact. I was into three's.....NO! ~ not a ménage trios! I was seeing three therapists at once.

I stumbled upon the Boston Graduate School of Psychoanalysis on Beacon Street in Brookline and met two nice therapists there. The first one was Thomas. He was of European decent and he had an accent that made it sometimes hard to understand him. He was in his thirties, ruggedly handsome, with thick jet black hair and had a soft, sweet charm. I could see how the girls would swoon over this one! I was very attractive to him, but he was much younger than me. I only go for older men. We got along fine until his superiors fucked up the whole therapy. He was great on his own but when he took his "case" with me to his superiors (which overlooked his workload of patients) they dictated what he should do and say and

it ruined the therapy. He was their "puppet".
And they pulled his strings. I was no longer
working with Thomas. I was working with
the men (his superiors) that controlled him.

After I told Thomas about my unorthodox
relationship with Dr. Love his superiors
wanted him to tape the sessions. I was
against this invasion and thought with a
tape recorder playing neither one of us
could act "natural". I started looking for
another psychologist, even though I had Dr.
Love and Thomas (two already). That's
when I came upon him – Dr. Jerry Kotch.
He was a psychologist at Children's Hospital
and also Dean at a local college at the time.
He was renowned in the country for his
many college text books and literature about
"ethics in psychology" He was a mastermind
in his field, a powerhouse at five foot three.
He was mine! I was only capable of getting
the college number. When I called
Brimmons and asked for him they gave me
his office number at the hospital. I found
his email address from the internet and
wrote him telling him all about my brain
damaged son, Alex. I knew he worked with
children and families who suffered

irrevocable catastrophic illness (like my Alex). I called his office and left a message on his machine. He called and emailed me back and we were set up for a first appointment....free of charge!

I was nervous as hell about this appointment. Maybe because it was at Children's Hospital and all the bad memories that it provoked about my son.........NO! It was something different than that. I dressed for the first session in a suit like I was going on a job interview and I brought my husband to the session as well. I have never (except for marriage counselling) had my husband come to a therapy session before. I told Dr. Love about him and he said Jerry and he were good friends. But he also told me that Jerry doesn't do "psychotherapy". He said he only works with terminal children and their families. Well, he WAS going to do psychotherapy with me! Wait and see!

It was January of 21012, a bleak, cold winter's day when I went for my first session with Jerry. I already had two therapists and he was now going to be my third! The session went off well. I was quite taken with

Jerry Kotch. He represented "power" to me. I am drawn to people in power. It was determined from that session that I would see him alone for therapy on a weekly basis at Children's Hospital in the psychiatric unit.....for children. Well what did I expect it was a "children's hospital". I was the ONLY adult doing therapy there, though he would talk with the parents that had children staying in the hospital. I felt sort of uncomfortable going in to see him every week when all the other patients in the waiting room were kids!

Around this time too I started writing poetry every day. I began writing my poems in 2011, but by this time I was quite serious about writing. I started emailing my poems now to Jerry. I was still drinking but writing poetry was helping me get all the buried feelings out, like purging the system of toxins. It was a catharsis of sorts. It wasn't working well with Thomas so I dropped him and found another therapist at the same place he was working The Boston School of Psychoanalysis. The new therapist's name was Ben, a black man in his sixties with whom I adore and still share my poems with on a daily basis to this day! So I was still toting three therapists, Dr. Love, Dr. Jerry Kotch and Ben. Three seemed to be the perfect number for me. I was totally honest with all of them. They all knew about each other, and none of them seemed to mind.

I was growing more and more attractive to Ben & Jerry....NO, not the ice cream, the two therapists. I would share my stories about Dr. Love with them, but mostly talked about Alex with Jerry. I was feeling everything was a good fit. I'm deeply into psychology and was doing therapy three times a week. Sometimes I would sit in the student lounge (at the Boston School of Psychoanalysis) waiting for Ben to have my session. They had a magnet of Freud on their refrigerator. I wondered what it would be like to be a student there. It felt like a second home to me. I would gaze at the syllabus on the door and see all the courses and professors listed.

Ben was the only therapist to make me lie on the couch, Freudian style, with himself behind me. I never felt right about this. I like face to face. I am a very visual person. But Ben and I had awesome chemistry that we didn't even need eye contact. I was growing fonder of him. He was dominant and aggressive and spilled out with charm. I believed he worked as a counselor as well in a high school but am not sure of this. He would never reveal too much about himself, just bits and pieces, one time saying, and I am quoting him here: "I'm a hard-nosed prick". I think after that session I just knew I loved him. He reminded me of Sidney Poitier in the movie "To Sir With Love". Every time I play that song that came from the movie I cry, missing Ben.

Though everything was going great with Ben it came to a final blow with Jerry. It was less than six months into the therapy. I walked in one session on a very hot, muggy June morning and Jerry said he had some bad news for me. He said he couldn't do therapy any more with me. I was devastated! He said it was the hospital's policy that he must be seeing only parents of patients that are currently in residence at the hospital. Since Alex hadn't been a residence at the hospital for over ten years he couldn't see me. He gave me a copy of the policy and said I could take a couple more weeks to transition out of the therapy. But I was numb. I just stood up, thirty minutes before the session was supposed to end and said I would be not coming any more. Then I parted with my last three words to him "I love you". I cried my eyes out and called Dr. Love right from the hospital. What would happen next would be a nightmare of cease and desist letters and heavy drinking.

Chapter 14 – Ben & Jerry

I thought it was so unfair and unjust of Jerry to tell me after six months that I couldn't see him, knowing all along that it was the hospital's policy that I must have my child be a resident at the hospital. Why did he even start treatment with me knowing this? This wasn't a new policy. It had been in the books for years. Now I realize that Jerry had a kind heart and wanted to reach out and help me, like Thomas did. It was only when Jerry's superiors looked over his patient load did they recognize what he was doing with me and had to put an end to it.

The more painful part of it though is I had a very hard time letting Jerry go. I felt abandoned once again and turned to drinking. I also was writing my poems and sending them to Jerry. I was so shaken up and thought I was treated so badly that I wrote a formal complaint on the consumer's complaints board about the situation, not particularly Jerry, but rather, that this policy was in effect when I started and I was still seen as a patient and then told after almost six months of treatment that I had to leave because of it when they allowed it in the first place.

I told Jerry about my complaint and emailed him a copy. He wrote me a rather cold email telling me he wants to stop further communications because he is no longer my therapist. Again, I was devastated and felt totally abandoned. It was bad enough I couldn't see Jerry but now he wanted to shut me off completely! I still kept sending him my poems though. Then one day I got this knock on my door. I had received a formal letter that I had to sign. It was from the Children's Hospital Security Department. How ironic, because I worked security myself! It was a cease and desist letter. In the letter the security from the hospital told me I must stop all communication with Dr. Jerry Kotch. If I didn't follow the letter as requested they would pursue legal action. I was in shock! This had never happened to me before! My heart was broken yet again, first by Dr. Love and now by Dr. Kotch.

So the summer of 2012 I spent my time with Ben discussing Jerry and all the pain he caused me. I was also seeing Dr. Love. I decided not to search anymore for a third therapist. I would have to make due with two!

It was an interesting summer. They were remodeling at the school of psychoanalysis, including all the therapy rooms. This meant that Ben and I got to go upstairs in the professor's offices to do therapy, which were much more lavish. Each week we were in a different room. One of the rooms was very formal with shelves and shelves of books and leather chairs and straight lined furniture, dark and sleek. Another room was soft blue and felt like being on a beach and lying on a lounge chair, open and airy. The variety of switching rooms was fun and the relationship with Ben was growing. I was getting really close to him. He helped me deal with my feelings with both Dr. Love and Jerry.

At this time I started a rather cheap and slutty affair with a much older man at work. Walter was in his late sixties. He was the overnight security officer. I was the morning officer that relieved him. But when I came in at seven to relieve him he would never leave.

Instead he stayed for an hour and talked to me during my shift. He never asked how I was doing or anything about me. All he wanted to do is talk about himself, which he had been doing for the past year. I was growing unhappy with the job. Most of the stores had left the mall. It was a ghost town by then. Then the mall got sold to new owners and had new management that did the security. I really wanted to leave, quit my job. But my husband at this point was out of work for two years, so that wasn't an option.

Walter tried to progress our "friendship" into a physical relationship. He was married too. He was the ugliest man I laid eyes on. He was bald, fat, practically toothless and an ignorant Italian. I never liked Italian men and he was no exception. He was so wrapped up in himself that he didn't care. At this time too, I was very sick with intense Gerd, so bad one time that I needed to be rushed to the E.R. for intense chest pains. I was on medication and worried also about esophageal cancer from my heavy drinking.

I don't know how I finally relented and started having oral sex with him but I did. I think it was because of the new security office's bathroom! They were remodeling the mall and they moved the security office into one of the vacant stores. It used to be an upscale boutique. In the back of the store there was a mirrored bathroom with a shower. Mirrors were, on the walls, on the door. My imagination went wild! I wondered what it would be liked to watch myself having sex.

So I guess I wanted "to watch" myself having sex so bad (like staring my own porn movie) that after months and months of nagging me I took Walter in that very bathroom and we got heavy into sixty-nine. This when I realized that Walter was impotent! But boy did he love sex. Men can orgasm even when limp. So all this meant is Walter and I would just stick to oral and never have intercourse. But let me tell you it is no fun to suck a limp dick. I was growing more and unhappy and Walter sensed this. So Walter got Viagra.

You guys think Viagra is a wonder drug? Think again! It did absolutely nothing for Walter. He took two, one before he came to work one morning and then one at work. We started fooling around...still limp! I was getting real angry at him. So I told him to take another, which he did. Then we waited. This was three now, when the prescription stated to take one pill. We started up again and still nothing happened! So I told him to take another pill and he said "but I took three already!!" But the idiot took it, four pills in all!!!~ still nothing, but he didn't feel right. A friend of mine told me he could have died taking that many!

My life was slowly going down the tubes fast. I knew I wouldn't last much longer on the job or with Walter and I needed to see a G.I. doctor because my condition was getting much worse. And I was still drinking! Then the worse news of all came. It was Ben. He told me that he got a new job as head of a clinic in New York. It would be a huge career advancement. It would also mean that he would have to move to New York which would mean he could no longer do therapy with me. Again, I was crushed!! I had just lost Jerry less than four months ago, and now Ben! And I needed help more than ever! All I had left was forty minutes a week with Dr. Love.

It was time now to buckle down and find a new psychologist. I looked though the list of doctors that was on my insurance. I came up with many different names. One I went to visit, but he was a smoker and his office reeked of cigarette smoke. And as soon as I told him I was seeing Dr. Love he told me I had to make a choice between seeing him or Dr. Love! Now who do you think I picked? Then I called "this one" Dr. James Dean himself, and my life neither has nor ever shall be the same again.

Chapter15 - Dr. James Dean

This was the day of infamy! Actually it was my son Austin that was born on December 7, Pearl Harbor day....the actual day of infamy. This was November 28th, 2012.....”Hangin’ around downtown by myself and I had so much time to sit and think about myself. And then there he was like double cherry pie. Yeah, there he was like disco superfly. Who’s that lounging in the chair? Who’s that casting devious stares in my direction? Mama this surely is a dream” I’m quoting the song “Sex and Candy” by Marcy Playground and you will come to understand why I chose those lyrics much further along.

This was an ordinary day and he looked like an ordinary psychologist and acted like one. But this was far, far, far removed from what one would call “the ordinary”. What I was about to enter into with him would basically change the molecules, change the structure of my DNA, throw me off orbit and into outer space and eternity would seem like a dream and ordinary life would seem surreal.

His practice was out of his home. When I
got there like a dumb –dumb I walked up
his front stairs to his house and looked
inside the door and rang the doorbell. I
should have known after all the different
shrinks I had that there is always a side door
they use for their office. So I walked along
the street and saw this little door. And on
this little door there was a little sign. And on
this little sign were the letters O F F I C E.
Hmm, I thought; maybe this is his office. I
opened the door and walked into a rather
large waiting room with enough chairs set
up to have a party. There was even a small
sink one could use as a wet bar! And then he
came out. He introduced himself and shook
my hand.

 He gave me all these forms to fill out and
handed me what seemed like a syllabus of
himself and his practice. Then I entered a
small room with two rocking chairs. I sat in
one and he in the other. He looked young. I
thought maybe thirties or forty, well fit with
dark hair, sporting a beard. He also looked
somewhat apprehensive and uptight. He
was sitting erect, at attention, with a
notepad and pen in his lap. He asked me

some questions, but not which vibrator I used! I thought it went pretty well, so I decided to make another appointment.

I noticed an email address in his syllabus. Great! I could now write him and send him my poems. So here is my very first email/poem to him:

Dean,

It was pleasant meeting you today. I wanted to give you a poem I recently wrote. When I got dressed today

I didn't know what to wear.

Everything looked dark and grey.

And life seemed so unfair!

I thoroughly searched my closet.

Looking high and low -

For an ensemble to composite.

To take me where I had to go.

Whatever I tried on -

It didn't look right in the mirror.

Before the time was gone -

I started to see a little clearer.

What I need is already at my disposal.

It resides right here, on my face.

A smile is always the best proposal.

And it's always in its proper place!

So I think I'll wear a smile.

It's easy and it's free.

It only takes a while.

And it sure looks good on me!

Here is Dean's very first email back to me:

Ms. Wyllie,

 Was nice to meet as well! Glad we will be moving forward with the continued evaluation!

Thank-you also for forwarding some of your poetic writing! It was helpful to have an example and a sense of your work! Have to say that I was impressed by your talent as well as by your sensitive and wise sensibilities!

Hope you have a better week ahead...and I look forward to seeing you next Wednesday!

Ms. Wyllie! My ass! Way too formal, and all those exclamation points six to be exact. Well, I'll be damned if I ever saw so much exclamations in one short email. But he seemed nice and I was happy I could write him and he would write me back.

I kept going weekly to him and Dr. Love. I was too afraid to tell Dean about Dr. Love yet. Since I was borderline he thought it would be better if I had DBT therapy or a group therapy. I didn't want those. I just wanted Dean! And I was staying put! I wasn't about to budge. But Dean can be persistent. He suggested the twelve step program of AA for me because of my drinking. But I knew I wasn't a real alcoholic just a very troubled person who used alcohol a little more than she should.

I went to a specialist for my severe Gerd and the doctor said I needed an endoscopy. I was really scared because they put you to sleep and put a long scope down your throat all the way into your stomach. I'm a real baby when it comes to anything like that. And I hate being "put to sleep". It sounds like killing a dog to me!

I would have never gotten through that procedure without the tender care that Dean gave me. He made me feel as though I could handle it. He said "You're not afraid to go to sleep at night; just think of it like that". It helped too, that I saw him the morning of the procedure. All I could keep thinking about was Dean as I laid there with the IV and a blood pressure monitor waiting for an eternity because the doctor was so late. I was starting to like this guy. And he had an adorable smile that made me feel as if I was in Vegas. When he flashed it everything lit up and his nose crinkled too. I finally had the courage to tell him about Dr. Love and he seemed ok with me seeing him. That was a big relief! I found myself talking more and more about Dean during my sessions with Dr. Love.

As the months went on I grew more compelled and intrigued by him. I felt something starting to shift inside myself regarding him. It's as if he was a great novel and I wanted to dive into it and keep going and going, never putting it down. I often analyzed him during the sessions and wrote and told him my thoughts from my analysis very bluntly and boldly without holding anything back. Here was one email that comes to mind:

Dean,

You can share all your worries and beliefs with me...and that is fine. It is not ok to use those worries and beliefs as an ultimatum for the treatment. When I went to my internist he told me I should to see the G.I. doctor for my stomach pains. He did NOT threaten to end the 17 year doctor/patient relationship if I refused. That's what you're doing. It is NOT some misunderstanding. I've been through this before with you. Trouble is your so damn good when you "relax" and "come off" your cheer-leader mentality. You have deep worries and doubts about seeing me and that is from your neuroses. Some of what you said was true about other therapists placating me. I've had ones that stood up to me as well as yourself. In fact I very much welcome that! I'm hell bent on making this work with you. I think when you talk to Dr. Love he will calm you...NOTHING ruffles his feathers. He is a good resource for you to have. He has stood by me for almost 8 years through thick and thin. What makes him good is that he LISTENS, and has the most perseverance and doggedness of anyone I know (except for my son). He believes in permeable boundaries and he does NOT do cookie-cutter therapy. Most of all he is confident.

I felt during this time (the first few months of treatment) that Dean was on the fence still if he actually wanted to keep me as his patient. He seemed very worried about my drinking and stomach problems and how I was handling things in general. I got fired from my job. I had been unhappy for some time there. I also dumped the idiot Walter that I was messing around with at work and I didn't know what direction I was headed in. I felt deeply scared that Dean was going to abandon me and end the treatment because he voiced many of his concerns with me. But I felt too that there was something very undeniable here between us that would carry the biggest change in both of our lives that we had ever seen. Boy I couldn't have known then how actually right I was about that!

No matter what kind of worries or disagreements we got into about my treatment Dean and I always worked things out. If Dean thought things weren't left in a good place he would invite me back for a "free session", one he wouldn't charge to my insurance. We would stay there in session, sometimes up to two hours until the matter was resolved and I left contend. I was thinking he was acting more and more like the old Dr. Love. He was showing that kind of care. Even when he no longer took my insurance we worked something out and Dean took a reduced rate.

Dean got to finally talk to Dr. Love over the phone. I'm not sure what they said, maybe they were comparing notes on me. But the real irony of this is that Dr. Love became Dean's psychologist and also did couples therapy for the both of us less than a year later. I felt an affinity with Dean. He was as neurotic and ballsy as I was. He wasn't afraid to speak up to me, as I wasn't afraid to speak up to him. And because of that we would often clash. We would have sessions where I would tell him that he's a hypocrite and insecure and neurotic. He would tell me that I needed a good swift kick in the ass. I even called him narcissistic one time and gave him a book on the subject! More and more I saw Dean as a mirror image of myself.

There was a growing attraction starting to occur as well. Before I went for my annual mammogram I asked Dean if I could take a picture of him to bring with me. He readily agreed to it. I carried that picture with me during my mammogram and throughout my days, even to this very day. I always have Dean with me. He's in my heart and has consumed my soul.

There was a point in the therapy I got stuck with Dean, even though we were still growing closer. For a while Dean felt ineffective with me. During each session I would rebuff any and all suggestions he would make. He had suggested during one session, because I love writing poetry joining "Stone Soup" a group of poets that gather for an evening in Boston. I didn't like the idea of traveling at night into town. He also suggested group therapy, along with the therapy I was doing with him. But I am a very private person and prefer the intimacy of one on one. I know he was trying to be helpful but because he was thwarted in all his ideas and suggestions it prevented him from being empathic. Sometimes I felt an underlying sense of hostility and aloofness from him.

One session in particular he recommended the book "Non-Violent Communication" and I called him a hypocrite because the book was about communicating in an effective, non-reactive and compassionate way. I did not believe that this was the way he was conducting himself with me. When I asked him how he was feeling he said "This is your therapy, not mine". When I told him he was a hypocrite he said "I'm at a loss" and then just sat there stone cold. I was quite upset and left that session in a huff.

The next session I came in Dean was quite different. He wanted to explain what had happened the session before. He said that he was too invested in my opinions of him, which was not enabling him to be as empathic as he could be with me. He became flummoxed and felt inadequate. My opinion of him mattered deeply. We both thought this session was a break through because we got to the underline cause of what was inhibiting a empathic response from him. I understood the importance and the weight that my opinions held and how they effected Dean. It was a major turning point in the therapy, as is always the case when the therapist owns his part too in the transference. Dean needed to work on not putting so much weight on my opinions and I needed to work on not being so critical and opinionated, something I still struggle with to this day!

Chapter 16 - Mama This Surely Is A Dream

"Hangin' around downtown by myself and I had so much time to sit and think about myself. And then there he was like double cherry pie. Yeah, there he was like disco superfly. Who's that lounging in the chair? Who's that casting devious stares in my direction? Mama this surely is a dream"

I started voicing my attraction to Dean and asked if it was possible to have more than a therapist/client relationship with him. In truth, by the spring of 2013 I was actually falling in love with Dean. At this time he admitted that he loved me too but more as a sister and not a lover. We were two kindred spirits carried off by the wind. There was something undeniable happening between us. With each session we were getting deeper and deeper into each other, and then Dean had a dream that would change everything. Here is the email about that:

Sandra!

Once again, appreciate your writing about last evening's session; your words and the images are really evocative and impactful! Likewise, glad that the session was meaningful and significant to you as well in such a positive way! An "epiphany" is a good word for what I had experienced after Wednesday's session and a "breakthrough" is what I would say I had experienced within yesterday's session as well! Moreover, I want to let you know that I had had a dream last night that I feel was very revealing about what had happened in the session, at least for me, and, while unorthodox, would like to share that with as well so that you might better understand the meaning of what has been transpiring between us for me and from my perspective! Would want to do so though in session rather than on line because of the complexity of the dream and the need to have the space to process its significance as well, but could talk on the phone sometime this weekend if that would be preferable for you! Let me know!

After receiving this email I told Dean to call me Sunday evening to tell me all about his dream. That conversation would change the relationship and draw us more closer than we ever could imagine at the time.

I waited anxiously by the phone for Dean to call that night. It was May 19, 2013, almost six months into the therapy with Dean. He called promptly at seven like he said he would. Dean was always punctual, something I greatly admire in a person. As soon as I picked up the phone he dived right into the dream. In his dream Dean told me we were in his office for an evening session and it was dark outside. There was only a soft glow cast by the moon coming through his window. As we were talking we heard what sounded like billowing, crashing thunder and the sound of hoofs gallantly racing into the night's cold, dark air. Dean and I went to the window, knelt down on our knees to have a look outside. What we saw astounded us both. The street had become a large field and stallions, hundreds of stallions were running free and wild by us. Then one stallion stopped right at the window and looked Dean straight in the face. His eyes were glaring and the horse's nostrils were flaring. And then Dean woke up.

That was far from the end of the conversation. We talked for three hours in all that night! I tried to open Dean up more about his personal life asking him questions that took him off his guard and after I was met with silence I told him he was in a bubble (Dean and I define the "bubble" as being shut off from what you are feeling, becoming inward) and he replied: "No, I'm not." "No one has ever asked me these questions before; this is my first time." I think I was asking him psychologically deep stuff at the time. I was trying to get into him. I had always told him that I had a fantasy of him lying on his couch with me analyzing him. He even told me that he would consider doing that. He said that this therapy was going to be unorthodox, just like Dr. Love's. That was an understatement! This would far exceed anything I had with Dr. Love, only we didn't know it at the time.

I tried to analyze his dream, of course. It was obvious that something quite powerful was taking over. Stallions running wild and free. Dean was wild and free. Dean was a rebel. He was a fighter. He had to be because his father use to beat him and he had to raise himself since the age of thirteen. He put himself through both high-school and college. He didn't know this but he was my hero. His spirit was one with the stallion. No one was going to saddle down Dean. I knew if I rode him it was going to bareback and I was in for the most bumpiest and wildest ride of my life!

Chapter 17 - Kindred Spirits

We had much in common, Dean and I. We were both Italian, both Catholics. We had both grown up in pain, with very abusive parents. We also had a deep spirituality and were both psychologically minded. Dean was starting to open up more and more in the sessions. I went into my session with Dr. Love telling him all about the phone call I had with Dean and how he shared his dream with me. I told him we spent three hours on a Sunday night talking on the phone. I also told Dr. Love he was signing his emails Love, Dean. I was too afraid to find out if Dean was involved with another woman. I was deeply in love with him at this point and that would hurt me too much to think of Dean with another woman, even though I was married myself.

Because of the struggles between us, Dean decided it was best to seek his own therapist. It is often such the case when a therapist is having his own internal struggles to seek therapy himself. Here is an email that Dean explicitly states such:

Sandra,

It is true that if something comes up for me in the course of working with someone that would compromise the work then I do need to seek consultation or some additional therapeutic work for myself! And with you this has certainly been the case; so I have actually already been thinking about and beginning to consider some possible options for the latter-- that is some further personal therapeutic work on the issues that had surfaced for me within my work and relationship with you! Hope that this is clarifying and confirming for you of my commitment to our work and to the health of our relationship!

With continued love, care and affection,

Dean

I was happy that Dean was addressing his own issues about me in his own therapy. Dr. Love said that there was definitely something going on with Dean concerning me. He said that no therapist signs his emails using the words "love", and he also said no therapist spends hours on the phone on a weekend talking to their patient or telling them about a dream they had.

I wrote Dean telling him what Dr. Love had said about some psychologists involvement with their patients. Here is that email:

Dean,

Consulted with Dr. Love today about us. He says there is "something there". He also has given therapy to psychologists who have fallen in love with their patients. He says he knows one that married his patient and has been happily married for over 20 years!! He knows of many more that have formed a romantic partnership with their patient...ended therapy to do so. They sought his professional help in this. He says I should "point out" ask you if you're in love with me!

 I NEVER will ask and I can't believe I'm even writing you about today's session with Dr . Love, but after last Wednesday I just needed to. This is a topic I NEVER want to discuss with you! I think Dr. Love is a romantic by nature and he loves me and wants what is best for me and I told him I'm in love with you! I can NOT handle your rejection....best for me NOT to know!

Love,

Sandra

Very soon after this Dean and I talked about my coming in twice a week. So I started coming On Tuesdays and Fridays instead of Wednesdays and Dean dropped the fee. He continually kept dropping the fee of my sessions. I also started sharing sexual fantasies that I had of him.

This was one:

Dean,

I want to fuck you in the rocking chair. Sit in your lap and ride your cock while rocking back and forth.

Love,

Sandra

Chapter 18 – Touch Me

"Now touch me, baby. Can't you see that I am not afraid" "Now, I'm gonna love you Till the heavens stop the rain" "I'm gonna love you Till the stars fall from the sky for you and I" The Doors, one of my favorite groups. Physical closeness follows that of emotionally closeness, so that the two merge as one, one uplifting the other.

As I was getting closer and closer to Dean the old "run-away" behaviors started to emerge and I would go through the motions of ending the therapy. Dean said it would break his heart if I left. During one session when I threatened to leave he clutched at his heart and tears were forming in his eyes. He said to me "I'd rather cut off my right arm". It was clear the significance I was having in his life. He said I challenged him. I questioned everything from why he needed to always have the note pad on his lap to why he would get reactive when I pointed things out to him like his neuroses.

During this time too because I was going twice a week to therapy I was getting acquainted with his neighborhood, getting to know people on the street. I met this homeless young man in his twenties named Myles. He was brilliant! I became fast friends with him. People often look down on vagrants. It's so sad because they miss out getting to know some of the most interesting people out there. Myles came from an abusive upbringing like me. He crafted jewelry and sold it on the street. I often bought his pieces, paying much more than they were actually worth to help him out.

There was an older black man in his neighborhood that worked out of a garage a couple of blocks away from Dean. He would always stand around the streets ogling at me. I never paid much attention to him until he started following me and pursuing me with a vengeance. I was afraid of him because he wouldn't take "no" for an answer. He kept following to my car too. I told Dean about him. I wanted Dean to talk to him, to tell him off, to come to my rescue. Dean was reluctant about this but offered to walk me to and from my car that was parked in the public parking, a couple of blocks from Dean's house and directly opposite the old man's garage. Dean later told me that he was personally struggling with whether he should talk to him.

I finally got the guts to stand up to this man myself, which I think Dean was trying to encourage me to do instead of relying on Dean to do it for me. I did this by imaging Dean as James Bond (I love BOND, big fan of the movies) and of course I was Bond's lover and assistant. He always had beautiful assistants! So I told this old man point blank to stop following me right in his face. After all James Bond's girlfriend would never be afraid to speak up. I stood there in the street, firmly in place yelling and pointing my "Gold Finger" at him for all to see and said "GO BACK TO YOUR PLACE!".

He turned and left fast, afraid to make a scene with people watching. Funny though, I am fast friends with AC (that's his name) to this day! I go and hang out in his garage, give him a big bear hug and shoot the shit with him, often opening up my private life to him.

During the month of August Dean and I discussed touching one another. It felt so natural because we were so very emotionally close. I was scared though. I was in love with him. I wondered what it would be like to hold him. He was very open to the idea. We had sessions and emails going back and forth on this subject. It was nothing that we rushed into.

And then one session it just happened. I didn't know it was going to happen that particular session. It was at the end of the session, and Dean asked if I wanted to....give it a try. So we both stood up slowly, looked softly, warmly at one another, with a little bit of trepidation made our way over to each other. And then it happened. I was ensconced in Dean's arms, taking him in, his musky smell, his tight firm body up close against mine. I felt like I was deep inside a woods. The walls were trees, the ceiling sky, his arms soft, feathered wings that which upon I fly. It's the poet in me. I never wanted to let go of him! It felt so good, so healing. I've never felt anything like that in someone's arms before. Of course the poet in me had to write him immediately about what it was I was experiencing in his arms.

Here is my poem about the first time I held
Dean:

I claim my innocence,

at my own expense;

Never before could

fathom what's in store,

how arms entwined

would love commence!

There before me

as I stood,

breathing in this musky,

Smokey cabaret out

in the wood

I clung to such a strong

and sturdy bark.

Felt exposed, indeed!

My fabric loose upon

the flesh felt so stark!

The sky it opened

when the thunder came.

With pulsing, pounding

rhythmic fever I danced

among the evergreens

without so much as

a twinge of shame!

I never knew the height

of the trees!

Standing on tiptoe I raised

myself to catch a warm

and tender, gentle breeze.

It was then the clouds bloomed

like roses to fill my head.

Floating, uplifting me safely

ensconced into a downy nest,

there laid my bed.

As I go adrift, I catch a doe

out in the mist, then...

Everything turns quiet,

s t i l l.

So silently I that I could

hear the softest landing

from the free-falling of a quill.

Now I turn my eyes inwardly,

for my sleep.

Into darkness pierces light,

for much this day that

I do reap!

And grateful too, to have

its secrets that I embrace, forever keep.

Chapter 19 - Kiss From A Rose

"Baby, I compare you to a kiss from a rose
on a gray

Ooh, the more I get of you, the stranger it feels, yeah

Now that your rose is in bloom

A light hits the gloom on the gray" lyrics to "Kiss From A Rose"

Dean and I ended each session now holding each other. I felt our bodies entwine as one. It was total paradise in his arms. All my senses were overflowing. The woodsy, musky smell of him lingered on me. The soft hair on my skin stood erect and alive while ensconced in his arms. His warm, soft hands caressed my back, while our pelvises drew tight toward one another. My spine tingled. It was electric! I wanted so badly to know the taste of his sweet lips on mine.

I told Dean in a phone call that I wanted to kiss him before he went away on vacation. After all, it would be a week that I wouldn't be seeing him. I tried very hard not to think of him in another woman's arms. How could he hold another woman after the way he has held me? And the thought of him going away with another woman was just too much to bear, though I suspected such. Dean also told me that he wanted to lend me a book on IFS therapy, something he was getting into before he left on his vacation.

The last session before Dean's vacation he presented the book to me with both arms extended, elongated out in front of him and the book resting right above his wrists. It looked to me as if he was cradling a baby. In fact it felt like we were fated to be together, that our love was "a calling". I accepted his offering as a sacrament, a rite of passage between us. As we both stood up simultaneously we made our way to each other. It felt bitter/sweet this time, as it was a departing. As we released our arms upon one another my lips met his and I lightly kissed him and then turned and walked out the door with the book in my hands. His vacation marked a turning point in our relationship.

Chapter 19 - Kiss From A Rose

I was so moved by what transpired between us before he left that I sent him this email while he was on vacation:

Dean,

I know from Friday what this is between us. We have a divine calling. It is a sacrament, a holy sacrament that we are called from God to receive. I knew the moment that you had "presented" me with the book, the way you held it cradled in your arms like a baby. It IS a baby, it is "our baby". That image of you cradling the book has been imprinted in my mind and now I feel it has become indelible and so is the sacrament and the divine calling we share.

I also know from reading the book (haven't finished yet) that when we are in true self (as we are when we hold each other) or as we were on Friday that there is a love so deep that it exceeds anything physical or even earthly. It is only when we are in our different parts (when we are reactive to each other) that it blurs the true sacrament between us.

And this IS a sacrament. It exceeds "therapy". It exceeds a "love relationship". It exceeds all. This is our true destination, our true calling! And the battered children inside of us shall be freed at last, and all the parts will be healed because the self will become so strong through this divine calling. I am blessed and you are blessed. I never felt so whole as I do right now.

Love,

Sandra

And Dean's reply back, during his Cape Cod Vacation:

Sandra,

Like the dream I had of us, I cannot help but share that as I began to read your message, there were two intense flashes of lightning and then an incredibly deep and billowing roll of thunder that virtually shook the building!

I am so moved and inspired by how you understand this work before us and what is transpiring between us! At the time, I honestly did not know why I was presenting the book to you in the way that I had; it was just happening and as it was happening, I was feeling taken aback by what I was doing! In so many ways, it was an unprecedented moment; and yet, in other ways...this being taken aback by what I am doing or saying or feeling with you...continues to happen over and again and to progress as well!

Moreover, the articulation of your understanding of what we are called to do and to be with each other does resonate deeply, even profoundly, within me I not only sense the transformative potential for both of us, but already feel that it is underway and happening! It is so good to hear that you are already beginning to experience the sense of wholeness that becomes available as you come more into Self and can sense the healing potential for the wounded and vulnerable parts that we carry between and within us!

 I know that what remains before us will challenge and test each of us...deeply and radically; and despite such and in some ways because of it, I cannot tell you how meaningful it is to me to undertake this work and this call with you...and how blessed I feel to know you and to be in this with you! I hope that you feel free to be in touch with me over this week if so moved...otherwise, I so look forward to seeing you again next Tuesday!

With much appreciation, love and affection,

Dean

Chapter 20 – Pleasant Valley Sundays

Soon after Dean got back from his vacation he suggested that I come to therapy three times a week. He wanted to try IFS with me and he thought because it was so involved and would evoke so much that we needed a third day as well. He was already working six days a week and booked solid, so he suggested that I come on Sunday afternoons from one to three. I readily agreed and was overjoyed to see more of Dean. Our new day and time would feel just like "magical Thursdays" did with Dr. Love.

Sundays were very different than during the week with Dean. He was always dressed casually in black jeans and sneakers and our time together was more laid back. I had recently started taking yoga at the new yoga studio a block from Dean's house. Dean had suggested it. He went there for yoga himself on Sundays and thought it would be good for me. I tried it out and fell in love with it. It had a spiritual and calming effect on me. During one of our Sunday sessions Dean and I did some yoga poses together on the floor. We had to move the chairs out of the way. I was quite impressed how flexible Dean's body was. He did rigorous work-outs like me and lifted weights as well. But he could bend his body in more ways than I never could!

The Sunday session even got more intense. For one session I brought in a blue afghan and a stuffed tiger. I laid the afghan out on the floor for Dean and I to sit on. I asked him more about his childhood and if he had any special toys or stuffed animals. He said no. I thought how sad. He told me he use to play ball out in the street with his brothers. So I gave him the stuffed tiger and told him to hold onto him. I told him he symbolized the tiger because of his fierceness. Dean also told me how bad his father would beat him leaving welts on him. His faced dropped and tears were starting to concentrate in his eyes. I put my arms around him and held onto tightly. It was a cloudy afternoon but something was burning brightly inside of me. I think I made a promise to God then and there that one way or the other I was going to protect, care for and especially love that wounded child deep inside of him.

Dean of course held me, and rocked me side to side before I left. I was swaying in his arms, as if we were dancing. I gently kissed him on the lips goodbye. This time he walked me outside. More often now on Sundays that's how we would end our time.

Because I was seeing Dean three times a week now including Sundays and going to yoga a block from his house I felt right at home in his neighborhood. It was like a second home to me. I was friends with the guys on the street there. I ate in the restaurants for lunch and shopped in the thrift stores all the time. But I had never seen his "private quarters" (where he lived) though, like I had with Dr. Love. I felt it was time now that I did. So one autumn day in October of 2013 when I was going to yoga I thought I would make a stop in on him and say "hi". I walked in the office door that led to the waiting room and up the stair into his home! I looked all around. I admit I did some snooping!

His home was painted bold colors of blue in the living room, green in the dining room, and a warm gold going up the stairs to where the bedrooms were. It was open and airy. He had two plants in the living room and a plain very light colored couch with two matching chairs from either Crate and Barrel or Pottery Barn, very clean lines. The fireplace had three different colored ceramic bowls on the mantel with an enormous one underneath. There was a huge ceiling fan, a straight tall floor lamp next to the couch on the right side. A shelf held many books as well as the coffee table. On the far wall was a piece of art work with many different colored pieces of wood. It looked like he collected many pieces of art work.

I went up the golden staircase. Actually the walls were golden, the staircase dark wood. There was a small table by a window witch sat a bonsai plant at the head of the staircase. And then I turned the corner and saw his bedroom of lavender! A big flat-screen TV was atop two weights. I was afraid he was somewhere close so I rushed out and the when I turned the corner there was a small bathroom with a clear door shower and then Dean's upstairs' office (not to be confused with the office he sees his patients in). I took a glance in and he was sitting at his desk staring at his lap top.

I had my yoga mat rolled tightly tucked tightly under my arm when I popped up and took Dean by surprise. He took off his reading glasses and immediately stood up. "I was just writing you an email" he said. I told him I was on my way to yoga and that I didn't have a stitch of make-up on. I always wore make-up to the sessions and Dean told me that he wondered what it would be like to see me without any. He came closer and looked at my skin, an touched me and said "You are beautiful; you don't need any make-up". Then he said smiling brightly "since you are here let me show you upstairs where I work out." So Dean escorted me up the stairs to a carpeted room in his attic which held a treadmill an a weight/press bench and a stereo. He had various weights in different sizes and yoga equipment. There were two sky-light roof windows, and a built-in bench looking out a window into the city streets below. It was lovely and quaint.

After "the tour" Dean and I went downstairs and he showed me around his living quarters. He said "What do you think; I painted and decorated everything myself" I told him I liked it. I then asked him if I could have a hug. We embraced and as we did I told him it was getting harder and that I wanted to truly be with him, as a woman in every sense of the word. He asked me "Give it more time; can you wait." I said in his arms, longingly looking into his soft brown eyes "I love you; you're worth waiting for. He walked me to the door as I set off for yoga up the street and as I turned to kiss him goodbye he said "maybe I'll do yoga with you sometime."

I was euphoric but also concerned and confused all at once. Was he seeing another woman? I know I needed to find this out. So the next Sunday as we were sitting on the floor I got him to talk about his past with woman. He never really last more than a few years with anyone. But there was this particular girl he was deeply in love with and he fondly talked about her. Then I asked, though I swore to myself I never would if he was seeing someone now. He said "Yes, but it's only casual". I was insanely jealous! How could he be holding and kissing me and at the same time be with another woman. I ran out of his office in deep duress. He chased me and pleaded with me to stay but I said "NO!" I have to visit my son." So he told me to come back afterwards in the evening, but I still said "NO!"

I rushed home and wrote him a "goodbye email". Here it is:

Dean,

I am ending this. I feel so cheap and used and hurt by you. I told you explicitly that when I learn that you are involved with a woman that I would end it. So I am just being true to my word. It should come as no surprise to you because I made this point VERY CLEAR to you.

I can't believe that you could hold me the way you did and love me while also doing this with another woman!!! It IS true! You ARE a womanizer. I should have known all along! I have NEVER held another man or loved another man as I had you. You don't last with any woman either, so it's no surprise that this one is on its way out.

The hurt I feel from this is so immense, much worse than Dr. Love. I think you are unethical the way you tried to use me through IFS therapy to heal yourself. I WILL NEVER ALLOW YOU TO USE ME LIKE THAT AGAIN!!! I'm sure it will take many, many years with a new therapist to even start to begin to heal the severe trauma you inflicted.

I will NOT be in Tuesday. I will leave your book in your mailbox, or porch, during the week some time when I expect you are in with a patient.

Sandra Wyllie

I did not speak to Dean or go to the next session. I was crushed and devastated. I don't know how he could possibly hold me these last few months and be loving another woman at the same time! He had betrayed me and I was hurt beyond compare. I started drinking heavy again and thought it was the end for good this time.

Of course Dean replied back to me as well as called me. Here is that email:

Sandra,

I'm sorry that you are feeling hurt by what I had revealed...and am concerned about how you are interpreting it and now refusing to speak. In many ways, I believe I can understand and appreciate why you are feeling hurt, but I fear that it is ultimately based in a misreading of the situation, which I am appealing to you to allow us at least the chance to address! I am concerned that you are blending or identifying the type of connection, care and love that has emerged in our relationship with a relationship in my personal life that is of a totally different sort. One has no real bearing on the other...and needn't in any way be a diminishment of or a threat to what exists between us! What you have stated in the past is that you believed that if I became involved with someone in my personal life that our relationship would end because I would lose interest in you and not care for or love you anymore! I challenged that contention over and again...and assert even more strongly now in this instance that it is not in any sense what has been happening...and I believe would never happen because of the nature of the unique bond that we share.

And the holding of you all along has come out of that bond, out of that deep place of connection, care and love...which we have both said over and again has been very real and true and more meaningful and healing than any mere romantic embrace...and I can't help but think that at some level you still know that to be true!

And I don't understand how I possibly could have used you through IFS. Because it has had personal value for me in addressing the challenges that have come up in our work together, I have wanted to share and use the model with you and to enable you the benefits of it as well...my wish to utilize it in our work going forward has come totally out of my desire to help you and has not in any way been about a using of you!

I will not fill the slot on Tuesday and I am again appealing to you Sandra to please re-consider this and allow us to address this situation together in person! Given what we have had and can still have, I believe it would truly be a tragedy to end our work and relationship in this way without even the chance of an opportunity to make sure that it is really well founded and truly the right or necessary thing to do!

Love,

Dean

I didn't show up the next session but I did break down and call him late Wednesday evening after skipping Tuesdays session. We talked until two in the morning. He told me that the relationship with his girlfriend was over. He said he didn't have the kind of deep, intense connection that he had with me. I told him he was falling in love with me and he said that could be a possibility, but that he was confused because he had never been in anything like this ever before. I told him that I would resume seeing him and come to my Friday appointment.

Deep down I knew I couldn't stay away from Dean. There was no point to be jealous of his girlfriend now or should I say ex-girlfriend. In fact Dean and I were getting closer and closer. Sometimes Dean would kneel on his knees by my chair just to be close. And he suggested we start holding each other at the beginning of the session instead of saving it at the end so we would have more time. He opened up to me more and more.

He said that the relationship he had with me was the deepest he ever had. I never experienced anything quite like this myself, even though I had a unique and unorthodox relationship with Dr. Love it would never reach the depths that I had with Dean. And this was just the beginning. I had absolutely no idea where I was headed, and really neither did Dean at the time. For our one year anniversary Dean bought me the book "Letters To A Young Poet" by Rainer Maria

Rilke. Inside he wrote a special dedication to me "To the most inspiring young poet that I have ever known, with love Dean. He said quoting Rilke, that "we must live the questions."

Chapter 21 – Love Outside The Boundaries

Nothing would prepare me for Black Friday of 2013 though. I told Dean that I didn't want to pay him anymore because our relationship was "personal" and NOT therapy any longer. I said this going out the door of my therapy session on Black Friday. He asked if he could call me that evening so we could speak about it. I told him that he could. After the session I went shopping. When I got home I washed my face and put my nightgown on and waited for Dean's call.

My Black Friday Poem:

It's the time of season for giving.
So much we wish to acquire.
Hurried past is the Thanksgiving.
And onto all selfish desire -
Harried rush to the stores.
Stressing out on what to buy.
Shoppers run amuck on the floors.
Heaving heavy with a sigh.
What foolish people do!
Not even minutely aware.
For all they so accrue -
They haven't themselves to share!

The gift that would befit -
It's not one with a price.
You certainly cannot buy it!
It comes from being nice.
A simple little thought -
As you rush about your day -
Doesn't matter what's been bought!
It's the niceness you convey.

Dean called promptly as he said he would.
We barely started to talk and Dean said "It's
hard to have this conversation on the phone;
can you come over?" Here I was in my
nightgown ready for bed with no make-up
on! But I still told him I would be right over!

I didn't even bother to get dressed! I
grabbed my car keys and told my husband
that Dean wanted to talk in person and he
said "at this time?". I suppose he was
already use to my seeing Dean on Sundays
which was highly unusual. But he did think
this was odd. I just grabbed my coat and
threw it over my nightgown. My heart was
in my mouth rushing over to Dean's house.
What would happen? What would he say? I
was so anxious! When I arrived I walked in

the office door which led to the waiting room. Dean must have heard me because he immediately came down.

He motioned me to go into his office. It was eerie, just like in Dean's dream. He put on a dim lamp but it didn't cast that much light. I took my jacket off and was sitting in my nightgown across from Dean in a very dim-lit room. I could still feel the bone chill cold on me from the late autumn night. Outside it was pitch black, except for the occasional street lights. I told Dean that the relationship was too personal and that I shouldn't be paying him any longer. Not only did he agree to this but he offered to reimburse me to compensate for any time in which I felt it had been this way. I told Dean I had no interest in taking his money.

We soon made our way toward one another. His arms enfolded me and I readily fell into them, eagerly awaiting whatever was to happen next. He then turned me around and sat me down on his lap in the rocking chair. He positioned his arms around my waist. I wrapped my arms around his neck. And then it happened; our mouths locked.

We had kissed many times before but this time he slid his tongue inside my mouth. It was so warm and inviting and I felt my whole body stir! I was alive for the very first time! I felt like a babe all wet and bloodied fresh from birth. But then Dean looked stunned, as if in shock. He said over and over "I crossed a line."

When you do cross that final finish line you can never start over again in the same race. This is a lesson we were about to learn. Although I continued for a few weeks doing "free therapy" this time it just wasn't happening. It wasn't real. I was no longer his patient. But then what was I, or rather what was I becoming to him ? The therapy had to end. Around this time too, Dean's psychologist lost touch with him. I think she felt too uncomfortable to continue with him in light of his feelings and the progression of the relationship he was having with me.

I was so confused and tormented and quite frankly worried what would happen next in this relationship. This was the very first time in my life that I was in love with someone who was in love with me too! It was fraught because I was his patient and I was also married. Dean was an ethical psychologist who never crossed any boundaries before. He also happened to be a very religious man who did therapy with priests and nuns. He never was with a married woman before. It was against everything he believed in to be with me! For the first time Dean wrote me a poem about how he was feeling. I think he beautifully captured it here.

Here is Dean's poem to me:

Up ended
Taken aback
Thrown forward
Beside myself
Brought low
Flying high
in a foreign land
that feels like home
Falling upside down
Where have I

ended up?

It is very hard for me to live with any kind of ambiguity. I always played things safe in life. I also had a deep-seated fear of being left abandoned that stemmed back from my childhood. I started drinking one night. I bought some vodka and mixed it with some pumpkin eggnog. I sprinkled some nutmeg on top. It was sweet and tasted good. I was starting to really feel it. I use drinking as a way to gloss over my troubles and to calm me down from the stresses of life. I was feeling rather psychotic though, having so much apprehension about Dean. When I'm in a "bubble" that means I'm shut down from my feelings or "turned off". When I'm "psychotic" that means that my feelings are to the extreme and I'm "turned on". Anything I'm feeling gets blown up to extreme proportions. This all/nothing stance is quite congruent with people who have borderline personality disorder.

It was a bitter cold December evening and I was feeling really blue and quite psychotic drinking my pumpkin martinis. I decided I needed to see Dean right now! I knew I was feeling those martinis but I didn't give a fuck! I got in the car and drove over to Deans. It is only a ten minute drive from where I live. I wasn't going particularly fast but I wasn't particularly "with it" either. I made my way around the rotary when I heard a sudden "crash". I was oblivious as to what happened and kept on driving. Then I noticed a woman in the car behind me following me all the way to Dean's house. I parked my car in Dean's driveway, and so did she. And then the police cruisers came and parked in Dean's driveway. This was all happening right outside Dean's office while he was still doing therapy with a patient!

The woman's car was completely caved in the front but my car had not even so much as a small scratch on it! One police officer questioned the woman and the other police officer came over to me. I thought this was it. I was going to jail for a DUI, and also for leaving the scene of an accident. I was sure they were going to pull me out of the car and give me a breathalyzer test. It was all going to be over for me this time for good! As the officer came over I rolled down my window. To my surprise he didn't ask me to step out of the car. He just said: "You can't leave the scene of an accident.' "She could have pressed charges and I would have had to arrest you and bring you in." Then he walked away. That was it, I thought. Both the police and the woman left. She was fine; she didn't get hurt. And I was off scot-free of what could have been the worse incident of my life leaving me with a criminal record.

I still couldn't believe that the police officer didn't know I was drunk. I got out of my car in a complete daze! I walked and walked all around Dean's house trying to find the door. I couldn't remember where the door was to get in his office I was in so much shock from what just happened. When I finally found it I walked into his waiting room. His office door was shut and he was still in with a patient. So I walked up the stairs into his home. I went upstairs to his bedroom and laid on his bed, dreaming of Dean and I together making wild and passionate love. I noticed a shirt hanging on his master

bathroom door connected to his bedroom. I grabbed the shirt and buried my face deep inside it. It had all of Dean's musky scent and body odors. I was feeling high from smelling it. I wanted to take it home!
Chapter 21 – Love Outside The Boundaries

I went through Dean's drawers and found just one pair of underwear. I proceeded to his bathroom off the hallway. A cologne bottle was on his sink along with shaving gear. I breathed the cologne into my nostrils. It was nice but not as real or as sexy as Dean's shirt that I took. That had Dean's real scent in it and not some artificial thing out of a bottle that any man could wear. I wrote down the name of the cologne anyway thinking because he was almost out and Christmas was only a couple weeks away I could buy him another bottle for a present.

Then I made my way into Dean's office. He had several bookcases with stacks and stacks of books on psychology, philosophy and religion. I went through all the patient files hunting down my own to read it. I did not go through any of the other patients individual folders. I didn't want to violate anyone's privacy. When I came across my own it was illegible, or maybe I was too drunk to read it! So I just sat at his desk and then I heard footsteps coming up the stairs! It was Dean! He walked in his office and had a look of horror on his face. He said "this is against the law; you're not supposed to be in here' "All my patients files are in here." I swore to him that I didn't look at any of them. Then he asked "what are you doing at my desk?" His lap-top was open but I didn't look at it or even touch it.

I broke down and told Dean that I had been drinking and drove over to his house drunk and got in a car accident and that I was pretty shook up. Dean's whole face changed and he became quite empathic. He said "let's go downstairs". So we walked downstairs, and I asked "you want to go in your therapy office?" but he said "no" and motioned me over to his couch. He was so nice. He asked if I wanted a glass of water or if he could make me a cup a coffee. But I said no. Then he turned his whole body around, lying across his couch with his shoulders and head resting on my lap and our faces together. We held each other this way and talked until I was sober enough to drive back home. We talked about our feelings of love and uncertainty and about our now very unique and challenging situation.

Chapter 22 – Living The Questions

I thought it was time to be open and honest with my husband and son about my relationship with Dean. I also didn't think it was really fair to still be having sex with my husband while Dean broke up with his girlfriend. It didn't feel right anymore either since now I was no longer Dean's patient but in this "limbo phase" of really not knowing who I was or how I was going to fit into Dean's life. Although at this point Dean and I were not sexual we already knew that we were destined to be. As Rilke said, Dean and I were literally living the questions.

My husband and my son were not surprised at all about this. They could feel something shifting between Dean and I, especially after the night I went to Dean's drunk and got in the car accident. So I thought all was well until I told Dean that I told my husband and son what was going on between us and that I was no longer going to have sexual relations now with my husband. Dean seemed very concerned about my decision and of course I took it as a rejection. I thought that since I wasn't going to be sexual with my husband Dean was looking at it as my trying to pressure him into sex which he was not ready for. Dean explicitly said "let's wait to have sex until we have a commitment." I knew I didn't want to wait because that is what I did with my husband (we were both virgins). I rushed into getting married in order just to have sex. I loved Dean and he loved me and that was good enough reason to me for making love. Again I got upset and Dean wrote me an email explaining his feelings:

Sandra,

 First, the issue again for me today was not about feeling pressured, but about feeling threatened as I had described, especially by the greater exposure of what is happening between us to the larger world in ways that I would have no control over. As I had indicated, I know that that is a trigger and a source of vulnerability for me, which I have to further work on!

Second, as I thought I had stated, I in no way would expect you to consult me about any decision that you would make, with regard to your husband or anyone or anything else! What I had stated was that I would appreciate our processing together any decision that would have potential implications or significant consequences for our relationship or for my life as well. Chapter 22 – Living The Questions

Third, I never said that I do not care about you're being sexual with anyone else, including your husband. I was only trying to practice acceptance around how you were handling that part of your life with him, having developed the impression that whatever was there was not emotionally significant to you and that I had further thought that it had been diminishing significantly over time as your feelings for me had been developing.
Also, having thought about it a lot since we met earlier, I know now that on an even deeper level, because of what the conversation today had stirred up within me, that I had not been letting myself really think about it, even blocking it out as some level, as a way to deal with it! This is

170

consistent with my only more recently allowing myself to fully feel my feelings for you; it's having been hard for me, as I have indicated earlier "to let myself go there!"

Love,

Dean

Things started really progressing fast after this. Dean was taking the week between Christmas and New Year's off so it was going to be the first time we really got to be together as man and woman and not therapist and patient. He invited me over for lunch one afternoon and told me to bring my yoga mat and dress for a yoga session, a private yoga session at Dean's house with Dean as the instructor! I could hardly wait!

I showed up promptly at noon and knocked on his front door. For the first time in a year of knowing Dean I got "front door status", no more small side office door. That was only for Dean's patients! Dean has this funny way of opening the door where he stood and hid behind it so that the door looks like it is opening on its own! It felt

171

really awkward at first after I entered. Dean
looked uncomfortable. Actually it felt like we
were two teenage kids and we didn't know
what the hell we were doing or getting
ourselves into for that matter!

Dean asked if it was ok to do the yoga first
and then have lunch. I told him that was
fine. So we walked all the way to the top
floor (Dean's work-out room in the attic).
Dean laid his yoga mat out opposite mine
and then proceeded to take off his sneakers
and socks and pants! He was wearing black
shorts underneath. It was the first time I
saw Dean's bare legs and his cute adorable
feet and small toes. He looked good enough
to eat up right then and there! I told myself I
must control myself! Dean would call me
yogi bear as a pet name whenever I was
doing my yoga.

I had taken several yoga classes at this point
so the yoga positions Dean would show me
were not foreign to me. We did downward/
upward dog and cat/cow and many, many
more. Dean would start out with a position
and I would follow suit on my mat. He was a
good instructor! I suggested he should teach

a class or two. We were there doing yoga in Dean's attic for one and half hours! That made us both really hungry! We had worked up an appetite.

So Dean put his pants and socks and sneakers back on and we went downstairs for lunch. He turned to me as we made our way into his living room and put his arms around me and then his mouth over mine, intense this time. Our tongues danced beautifully together and I was feeling quite euphoric. I could also feel Deans pelvis press against mine and what I notice to be a bulge developing in his pants. He parted his lips from mine for just a moment to ask me what I wanted for lunch, salmon he had left over that he bought at Wholefoods or the chicken and bean dish he made. I, of course, said I wanted the chicken because Dean made it himself. I spent a lot of time with Dean that week.

I had been nagging Dean for a while to get a real Christmas tree. Dean said because he lived alone he never got one. So one day to my surprise Dean got one and strung it with cobalt blue lights (his favorite color). He made me close my eyes when I came in and "viola" there was his tree by the windows across from the couch. It didn't have a single ornament on it or a star or angel up top of it, just the cobalt blue lights. It was perfect! Dean and I spent many evenings sitting on the couch gazing at the lights dancing on his tree.

It was New Years Eve of 2013. I spent the day over Dean's but went home that afternoon. I don't really do much for New Years. I didn't ask Dean what he was doing either and it made me conjure up all these fantasies and jealousies of Dean with another woman. So I wrote Dean an email asking what he was doing and he didn't write back. We never discussed New Year's Eve. I then called his cell phone and it went right to the answering message. I was starting to panic thinking of Dean with another woman. It was getting later in the evening around eleven- thirty, thirty more minutes it would be midnight and a new year – 21014!

I was in a frenzy (my psychotic state). So I hopped in the car and rode over to Deans. I needed to know what he was doing and who he was doing it with! I pounded his door when I got there. It was totally dark inside, peering through his window. He wasn't answering, so I called his cell phone again. I'm thinking he's at a swinging party with another woman about to kiss her as the clock strikes twelve. My blood is boiling over at this point! Then in the dark haze I see Dean make his way to the door. He is unkempt; his hair is tousled and he looks in a daze. He opens the door and says "what are you doing here; it's late." I said "you didn't answer your phone and I thought you were out with another woman". So he motions me in his house and turns on the light. He said "I went to bed early." But it was New Year's Eve, how could he not welcome the new year in?

So he didn't go out; he stayed home. That was clear. Then who was he with? I ran up the stairs to his bedroom. There had to be a reason for his going to bed early and I was going to find her! I got to his bedroom but there was no one there, just ruffled blankets and scrunched up pillows. I was feeling quite devilish and filled with wanton desire. So, I thought, if there is no other woman in his bed than I shall be the woman in Dean's bed. I took all my clothes off and laid there stark naked. Dean came in and said "what are you doing; you took all your clothes off?" I pulled Dean down on the bed with me. We started to kiss. Dean kept saying over and over again "this is so surreal."

He never kissed me with such ferocity as this before. His mouth suctioned down on mine. His tongue ran over my gums until it met my tongue. Then our two tongues entwined like snakes mating in the grass, coiled up and hissing. His hands found my soft mounds and gently caressed each breast as his mouth hungrily made its way to my erect nipples and pulled on each one with his teeth until they were standing clear up to his ceiling. I hungrily pulled his shirt off and ran my hands through the soft downy hairs on his chest. I could feel his tight stomach and each taut muscle of his six-pack. I was moaning low as my body was rising off the bed. I pulled his shorts off in fell swoop and stroked his bulging stiff erection. It was more than I could bear. I had to taste his manhood. So I went down and took his smooth, slick cock in my mouth and started sucking and sucking real hard. I could see on his face how much he was enjoying it. But then he pulled my head off.

He laid me flat across the bed and said "I want to taste you". I was beyond myself, outside myself, into another hemisphere. His tongue darted in and out of my pussy, all around my swollen clit, which was now on fire! Then he stopped all of a sudden, right before I was about to burst and took his stiff cock to my pussy. He just grazed over the hairs, tickling me. I want to pull him deep inside of me, but he wouldn't allow this. He suddenly stopped and laid back again saying "this is so surreal". I wanted to fuck him right then in there. He turned to me and said "it's only been a few weeks since you've been in my office, since you've been my patient."

I was real disappointed. Did he have to leave it this way? I wanted to stay the night but he refused saying "what would your husband say?". I felt so frustrated as he started to get dressed. It felt as if first, we were totally ensconced in loving one another and now we were acting like total strangers who just woke up next to each other after being totally drunk the night before. I couldn't help but show my disappointment. Dean apologized for disappointing me and said we should talk. So we went downstairs and sat on his couch and tried to put the pieces together. But we couldn't really. We had seen the New Year in, a year to come with many questions......

Chapter 23 – They Meet

I knew that I had some higher purpose in Dean's life than to just be his lover. I felt God put me specifically in his life for a reason. At this time our relationship was going outside the boundaries and defying everything that could be or ever should be between a therapist and a former patient. I felt really bad that Dean tried to seek help over his struggles within our relationship only to be abandoned by his therapist. I also knew in lieu of our unique and special situation that if Dean ever did seek the help of another psychologist he could be placing himself in grave danger. I knew that there was only one person who would understand who would show him the kind of compassion and care that he needed at this time. That person was Dr. Love.

I had been doing therapy all along with Dr. Love and spending the whole therapy just talking about Dean and I. So it was not foreign or out of left field for me to ask Dr. love for help concerning Dean. Dr. Loved was booked solid so I offered up my therapy time for Dean to see him. Dean thought it would be better if we both saw Dr. Love together, since the problems arising were between the both of us and operating out of our unusual situation. I told Dean to spent a few sessions first getting to know Dr. Love one on one and that I would be ok forgoing my therapy time for his sake. So Dean agreed he would go solo for a few sessions and then I would join him. Dean was going to start on Monday seeing Dr. Love. The two shall meet! It was all mixed up now. I had two psychologists doing psychotherapy. Now I had a boyfriend I was dating and a couples counselor who use to do psychoanalysis with me doing couple's counselling instead with my new boyfriend who use to be my psychologist!

The next evening was a Sunday and Dean I are were going to go out on our first "official date". He was taking me to Masona Grill in West Roxbury. I really overdressed for the occasion but I wanted to look my best it being our first date and all. He was going to pick me up at my house! I know that's unusual given the fact that I'm married and my former psychologist was coming to my house to take me out on a date. Of course I had to meet him outside; I sure couldn't invite him in to meet my husband and son!

I wore a long, low-cut floral satin dress and Dean was dressed in black jeans and a tee shirt. He said "it looks like you're dressed for a night out on the town!" But I like to dress up and look pretty. I had never been to Masona Grill before, even though it was in my backyard and now I know why. The prices on the menu were very expensive! We walked in and were seated right away because Dean always made dinner reservations. No matter how early he would take me out or how empty a restaurant was Dean always made reservations. And Dean would always pick out the restaurant too. This I didn't mind because I'll eat and drink about almost about anything!

Dean ordered some Pinot Grigio for the both of us as we looked at the menu. Dean and I usually split an appetizer before the main course and we almost never order dessert. Now I have a sweet tooth and love desserts but Dean doesn't do well with sugar or gluten or red meat. He has a rather restricted diet. We split the smoked salmon for an appetizer and I had the seafood paella, which was rather good. Before our entrées came Dean kept saying again just how surreal it was to be out with me, a former patient. I figured after New Year's nothing should feel odd anymore. After all we had seen each other totally naked and had been quite intimate with one another. Dean made his way over to me and sat next to me. I was sitting on a bench and he was in a chair across from me. He started kissing me right there in the restaurant! How passionate! I don't think anyone has ever done that before with me.

The evening went along fine and the next day was Monday, which was going to be Dean's first session with Dr. Love. Dean told me that he would call me that evening to let me know how things went. I was so excited and happy for Dean to finally get to meet Dr. Love. I had spent so much time talking to him about Dr. Love and our very special relationship that we shared. Now Dean was not only going to meet him but he was going to get to experience first-hand for himself just how good Dr. Love is as a therapist!

Dean went that morning, during my time slot and saw Dr. Love. He wrote me an email telling me that he thought it went well but would call me that evening to give me the details. I couldn't wait to talk to Dean. Dean said he would call me at eight, and as always called me promptly on time.

We started talking and Dean told me he discussed with Dr. Love how very hard it is for him to be with me because I was a former patient. He said Dr. Love was very understanding. He further told him about New Year's Eve and how things turned sexual and that he wasn't ready to take it to that level yet. He wanted some time to process things.

As Dean was talking I felt myself getting more resentful. I truly wanted Dr. Love to help Dean but Dr. Love was my psychologist of nine years and I was giving up my only time with him to help Dean and I had no one else to turn to now! Dean unknowingly went on to talk about his fear that if I moved in with him and it didn't work out we would be stuck. At the time I had no job and therefore no means to support myself. So if I left my husband I would be leaving my only means of financial security as well. I felt myself growing more and more psychotic as Dean was saying this.

I told Dean if I was to move in with him and it didn't work out that I would have no choice but to report him to the board. After all I would be giving up everything for him, my home, my security, my son. I would have no other way of supporting myself. What was he going to do, throw me out on the street? I'm sure by then my husband would have changed the locks on the doors and have filed for divorce. My husband was growing more upset with me seeing my former psychologist and at the same time denying him sex! Dean started really worrying. He had no idea I would even entertain about going to the board. I spent hours on the phone that night with a very angry and shaken up Dean. I wrote him an email the following day about that phone call:

Dean,

The shit hit the fan last night because of everything that has been bottled up and held so tightly internally within us both. It does no good to point fingers or lay blame. We are both hurting and struggling and fearing the other. I think last night was an accumulation of insecurities and fears and hurts. Relationships are very hard work if they are going to work out at all. And what we are up against increases that tenfold.

That phone call would change the way Dean related to me. It's as if the bubble burst that night. Dean continued to see Dr. Love for the next couple of sessions and then it was time for me to come to do couple's therapy. I can't explain just how weird it is to have both of your psychologists with you at once, though one is a boyfriend now and the other is doing couple's therapy instead of individual therapy. And it is also highly unusual to see your former psychologist as a vulnerable patient with many foibles himself. To this day it unnerves me!

I must say I was very impressed with the way Dr. Love handled couples therapy. He was impartial and empathic to both of us at the same time. He was helpful too. I was seeing him in a new light. It felt strange and good at the same time. He had a new role in my life and I was no longer in love with him now. I was in love with Dean and trying to make this work out. But Dean and I had a sex problem as well. Dean would freeze up in bed. I think he still couldn't get over that I was recently his patient. At the same time he was very worried that I could destroy his life. If I was ever to go to the licensing board it would be all over for him. Sex with a patient is always unethical under any circumstance. The best you can do in a situation like ours is to wait two years without any contact with one another. That seems so unreasonable! Yet that is the law and the way they wrote it up.

I continued hard to try to have intercourse with Dean. I succeeded in only giving him blowjobs. I loved his hard cock in my mouth. I would take it deep down my throat and swallow every last bit of his cum. He would shake and scream in ecstasy, sometimes digging his fingernails deep inside my flesh with each spasm! Even though I relished in each blowjob I gave Dean until my eyes were tearing and my mascara running I still yearned to be one with Dean. I wanted his body joined inside mine. He tried real hard but there was some psychological block there.

There were times I would get so upset at Dean that I would get out of his bed, get dressed and run out his front door with Dean following behind me. He would chase me down his very busy city street begging me to come back. I don't know what his neighbors thought, or for that matter the crowds of people who walked by us! I even got so mad that I called my husband to come get me a couple of times!

The stress surrounding sex was at an all-time high at this point. It had been two months into the relationship and one night I just about had it with Dean and exploded telling him "I will not be in a celibate relationship!" I gave him an ultimatum before he drove me home "either we have intercourse or the relationship is over." I told him to think it over.

As Dean was driving me home I was getting into a rage and feeling more and more psychotic and angry at Dean. I open the car door and shouted quite angrily "YOU FUCKED ME OVER". Then I slammed the door and headed for my house. Dean yelled out of the car window "Sandra, come here; let's talk." I turned around and got back into Dean's car. I told him I would not continue any longer like this. We sat there talking on my quiet dead-end street and I'm thinking the whole neighborhood is going to know something is up with the yelling and slamming of the car door. And Dean was still parked outside my house!

I told Dean that we should go back to his house (even though we just came from there) just to have a place to talk. So Dean drove back in a daze. When we got inside his house he was still in daze and just stood there with his jacket on looking dumfounded. I tried to get him to talk but he wouldn't even look at me. He said "you told me you were going to give me time to think it over." I didn't tell him how much time. Maybe he was thinking days and not minutes! Then Dean took me by the hand and led me upstairs. I said "where are we going?" We headed straight to his bedroom. We started kissing and going at it again. But this time things were different. He put his penis deep inside of me. I couldn't believe it. He kept thrusting and thrusting and as he did he said "it never felt like this before". But I got really bullshit the next morning sending him this email:

Dean, I was wondering how you maintained yourself last night. My perception was that you could all along but when it came down to losing me you made yourself available for it. And what I suspect is that it was more of a "control issue"....than a "jam".....using sex as a weapon for control.........because last night proved it (in my eyes). It IS sadistic to DO that!!
Maybe I'm wrong, but how else would you explain your performance last night??

I also sent this nasty poem along with that email:

Start the engine up, start the engine up.
Don't let it stand idling.
You know what they say, what they say.
You're gonna kill it with your stifling.
A little back and forth, a little in and out,
you're the control shifter.
Fuck the bottom out, fuck the bottom out.
Put it in reverse as you lift her.
Take her for a ride, Take her for a ride,
getting drunk from speeds that high.
You're cruising for bruising, cruising for
bruising.
Slap it hard; don't leave it dry, don't leave it
dry!
Her mouth is on the stick, mouth is on the
stick.
Now, who has the control, shit......her!
You nasty little prick, nasty little prick,
Control Shifter.

WOW! Looking back on this I feel like such
a bitch. It's really not a nice way to
remember your first intercourse! But it was
so fraught as the relationship was because of
the extreme circumstances we were both in.
In fact I should have saw how hard Dean
was really trying.

Dean thought it best that we both see Dr. Love individually and as a couple. So when an afternoon slot opened on Mondays Dr. Love gave it to Dean. But he also charged him two hundred and twenty-five dollars for it! In the mean time I was seeing Dr. Love Monday mornings for free! And during Dean's very expensive session he would allow me to come to do the couple's therapy as well. Dean was sacrificing a lot here. He didn't charge what other psychologists did so he wasn't making half of their salary. What he was paying Dr. Love out of his own pocket (Dr. Love didn't take insurance) was really hurting Dean! Dean worked in an urban area with low income patients and he wanted to be accessible to people, unlike Dr. Love who worked in a upper-class neighborhood.

Chapter 24 – I'm Alive

True self and false self are concepts
introduced into psychoanalysis in 1960 by
D. W. Winnicott. Winnicott used "True Self"
to describe a sense of self based on
spontaneous authentic experience, and a
feeling of being alive, having a "real self".
"False Self" by contrast Winnicott saw as a
defensive facade - one which in extreme
cases could leave its holders lacking
spontaneity and feeling dead and empty,
behind a mere appearance of being real.

You know your met your soul mate because
they are the one to bring you "into being",
not just living and breathing but truly being
alive. Dean was my muse and what I
experienced through Dean was making me
emerge as if I was going through the dark,
bloody watery existence of the womb and
out into the stark, vast world of light. This
can only happen when you come into being.
I am an intense and passionate woman who
unfortunately has been suppressed all of her
life. Part of this journey of being alive

involves taking risks and going way outside your comfort zone.

By the spring of 2014 I was willing to leave my family and home and share a life with Dean. But Dean did not know what he wanted yet. He had been a bachelor and lived on his own his whole life. We had many walks and talks in the arboretum. Every Sunday afternoon Dean and I would go there and walk among the lilacs and cherry blossoms, soaking up the sun and having very deep and intimate discussions. The discussions sometimes could get heated. But I remember fondly one time the two of us sitting on a bench in the shade pledging vows to one another. I started first, got down on bended knee and solemnly swore never to go to the board if the relationship were to end. And Dean made the promise that if things were not to work out between us that he would never abandon me, that I would always be part of his life. This was a very special moment and one I hold sacred.

Yet there were inflamed times at the arboretum as well. One in particular that comes to mind was on Dean's Memorial day vacation. Dean works very long hours, seeing nine patients a day. By this time Dean was feeling burned out. He wanted badly to go away on a private, spiritual retreat during this vacation but knew I would be upset and feel abandoned if he were to leave me.

During our walk I was sensing a rage building inside of Dean. He brought up about wanted to go away and how I wouldn't let him and he said with his face awry and scornful "you want to control my life". He was pacing now like a madman. I told him that he was emotionally crippled and was looking for a mother figure and not a girlfriend. The conversation was starting to get loud and real heated. I was worried what the children and elderly people would think passing by. Then Dean turned to me and said "FUCK YOU". I never had anyone swear out loud to me before in public. Dean was pacing now and I was growing scared of him, scared enough that I was entertaining the idea of calling the police.

I told him to leave me alone and go home, that I would get home myself. I only live minutes away from the arboretum. He said "no". I kept telling him to go and he kept saying "no". Dean can be quite forceful and dogged at times. I eventually softened and allowed Dean to talk with me, but it was nearing the time I had to get my son so we had to cut it short. Dean said he would pick me up after my son left so we could go back to his place and talk some more. The rest of that afternoon I grew more and more upset with Dean and by the time he came to pick me up again I was full of rage.

We got back to his place and he said that he was burnt out because he didn't get any relaxation during his vacation and how much I could destroy his life if I were to go to the board. He also said that I always criticize him and that nothing he does is ever good enough for me. I thought that he was "going off" on me again so I bolted out his front door with him running after me on the street, begging me to come back. This was a common reoccurrence, this running out his door and him chasing me down the street. Eventually I went back inside and we talked it over and kissed and made up.

Dean had a "breakthrough" about what provoked him so much that Sunday and he told me the following Sunday at the arboretum. He said that he was having transference, depicting me as his father. One time when Dean was a little boy he ran off and when the police brought him back home his father made him take all his clothes off and lay across the bed naked and then whipped him severely with a stick, leaving large welts on him. Dean swore he was going to die and prayed to God real hard that he wouldn't.

I reminded Dean of his father, because just like his father almost killed him, so could I destroy Dean by reporting him to the licensing board. It was understood what was happening and about the transference. We discussed this in couple's therapy with Dr. Love. We also found out that Dean wasn't the only one to carry the transference, but I was as well. I saw Dean as my abusive mother. So there was this cross transference of such that was triggering all these wounded child-like parts (IFS at work here). We had better insight now into what was happening, though it was a long road ahead with many more bumps and bruises!

I was having trouble sleeping. I had severe insomnia, unlike I ever had experienced in my life before. I would see EVERY hour of the night, not an ounce of sleep. Everything was just "over the top" for me. Sometimes when I felt so drained from all that I could not control in my life I felt like I was having a nervous breakdown. I would call Dean up and tell him I was so scared of that happening! Dean would allow me to come over to his place and crash for the afternoon while he worked. It was restorative for me. One time I got some books out of Dean's study and brought them into his bedroom, put on one of his shirts with all of his smells in it and lay down in his bed and read. I felt right at home at his place.

Through the good, the bad and the ugly I was "alive" with Dean. I never experienced anything like it before. He had this sporty convertible and one night in the bone chill of winter I asked him to put the top down. There was snow everywhere on the ground and it was freezing cold. But the stars shined so bright that night driving around town with my bad boy and the roof top down, wild and free! Now that's feeling it! That's being alive! Even the fighting was electric. It was passionate. We both were also very committed to making this work.

During his May vacation we climbed atop Blue Hills in stone silence (yet another argument) and when we reached the parking lot I swore I wanted to end it because I didn't feel like I was important enough in Dean's life. He didn't take me away on vacations like he did with all his other girlfriends. I never even spent one overnight at his house. When I said this Dean broke down and cried saying "you're the most important person in my life".

Chapter 25 – Summer Of Our Discontentment

It was another Sunday but this one was very rainy so we couldn't do our usual walk in the arboretum. Dean picked me up and suggested we go shopping! To a mall! He suggested the all at Chestnut hill where I use to work. I felt a little uneasy when he brought that particular mall up because I didn't really leave on good terms. But I didn't say anything. Dean said he was looking for some shirts, so we hunted around Bloomingdales but he couldn't find anything he liked. He liked matte colors, mostly in blacks, charcoals and browns. He dressed very down, and plain. He never wore anything except a shirt and pants, no rings or watch or even underwear for that matter! He was quite stark in appearance!

We started heading toward the main part of the mall and I was feeling quite flooded with memories of when I use to work there, unbeknownst to Dean who was on a hunt for shirts. He spotted Crate and Barrel and said he wanted to look in there as well. He said he needed a soap dispenser for his kitchen.

So of course we look at all the soap dispensers and Dean finally found one. He paid for it with his credit card. Dean never has any cash at all on him. He asked if I wanted to look at any other stores, but I said "no". I just wanted to get out of that mall! So Dean suggested another shopping area relatively new to the area and we went there to look for his shirts. He saw some he liked and I went in the dressing room with him as he tried them on. Now I badly would have liked to give Dean a blowjob in the store dressing room. But Dean was a man on a mission to find shirts. Well James Bond was on plenty of missions too but that never stopped him!

We looked around some more and made our way into Pottery Barn. Dean saw this lantern he really liked. He said he would like to get it for his coffee table but he was on a mission for sneakers this time so the lantern would have to wait. His old sneakers were falling apart. The very next day I went back to Pottery Barn and surprised Dean by buying that lantern. I had them wrap it up in a big box with a long brown ribbon.

Dean and I headed toward the Dedham Mall
area and I suggested DKW to look around
for his sneakers. Again he asked if I wanted
to look at anything myself or wanted to stop
and grab a bite somewhere. I knew the time
was getting late and that Dean was on a
mission to get shirts, then the soap
dispenser and now sneakers! And sneakers
he found!

I went home thinking how self-absorbed
Dean was! I have never seen a man occupy a
day shopping just for him. Although he did
ask if I wanted to look at anything I just
knew he was only saying that to be polite. I
believed all along that Dean could be very
selfish and quite self-absorbed. Why if it
wasn't for Dr. Love Dean wouldn't even
recognize this because every Wednesday
when Dean picked me up he would take me
grocery shopping with him. I could not
believe this! Why would I have to go around
with him when he was doing his food
shopping on a night he was supposed to

spend time with me!! He eventually chose another time to do this.

Dean and I got into yet another big argument about the "shopping spree" with Dean called me a two-face, holding two of his fingers, the index and middle one up to his face being as demonstrative as Italians are! He said I went along with it and then I grew to resent it. Well that might have been our first and last shopping expedition for a while!

The next Sunday was sunny so we did our usual walk around the arboretum. Dean had been feeling down about turning the big 6 0 in October. He said he felt like he was treading water and that men half his age were accomplishing things and making the kind of money that Dean never had. I would listen to him and try to encourage him to explore more territory. I myself was working on collecting all the poems that I had written over the past few years and putting them in a book. My first book to ever be published "Poems From Within". Everyone needs to reinvent themselves from time to time.

I was worried that Dean was having an "identity crisis" unable to define himself and his worth in this world and that I was being swept up in it. I didn't want to be part of Dean's crisis, like a married man having an affair when he hits mid-life. I wanted to be a permanent part of Dean's life. Although Dean was booked solid he took out an ad in Psychology Today's Website and went to CVS to take pictures for his new profile. On that public profile Dean could write who he was and what he believed in and the responses back would build up Dean's confidence.

Soon enough though something came along to really lift Dean's spirits and give him something new and meaningful to strive for. The Archdiocese wanted Dean to do a work-shop about stress among priests. Dean had worked with many priests in his therapy practice and he himself lived in a monastery when he left home at seventeen. He was a man of deep spirituality and solitude. Dean had very high religious convictions and didn't even lose his virginity until he was twenty-six years old, which is exceptionally late.

I was so happy for Dean and it changed Dean's whole attitude and outlook on life. He was no longer "treading water" but now he was focused on a talk he would be giving and a paper that he would be writing, the very first talk and paper he had ever done. I told him that he should talk to Dr. Love about this because he had given countless speeches across the country and written extensively. Dr. Love even wrote about the session where I stripped completely naked for him, offering him a blowjob!

Though I was happy for Dean I realized that this "project" would be putting a lot more pressure on Dean. He already worked eleven hour days seeing patients and then there was the pressure about our relationship building. At this point I had told Dean that he had to finally decide if he wanted a true commitment with me. My husband and son were extremely upset about our "fling". And I did not want a fling, or something casual. I wanted a full commitment! I told Dean that after one year of going out with me he needed to decide whether he wanted to spend his life with me or not. And if he couldn't decide or didn't want to commit then I would end it. Dr. Love thought this was the only fair thing to do. I couldn't keep going on being Dean's mistress. I felt used. Dean never introduced me to his family or his friends. I felt like I was just going to end up a skeleton in Dean's closet. The pressure was ratcheting up until it was beyond what Dean could cope with.

Chapter 26 – Bat Out Of Hell

Nothing ever grows
In this rotting old hole
And everything is stunted and lost
And nothing really rocks
And nothing really rolls
And nothing's ever worth the cost
And I know that I'm damned
If I never get out
And baby, I'm damned if I do
But with every other beat
I got left in my heart
You know I'd rather be damned with
you....Meatloaf

Because of all of the pressures that doing
this workshop put on Dean he was feeling
very anxious and getting easily tired and it
was starting to wear on the already unstable
and volatile relationship we had. There was
a particular night in September where
everything came to a final blow. Dean was
already thoroughly exhausted. He picked me
up Sunday evening after my son left and we
drove back to his place. When we got inside
barely before we even sat down I turned to

Dean and said "I feel insecure in this relationship." Dean immediately became enraged. He said I always put him down and always find something wrong. I just wanted to express my feelings and all the insecurities I felt in this relationship.

Dean was working himself up more and more in a tizzy. I turned and headed toward the door saying "this was a mistake to have come here." He headed toward the door and blocked it, preventing me from leaving. So I made my way to the side door but he blocked that as well. Then I went back to his front door but this time he grabbed me quite forcefully and threw me down on the couch. He was screaming in my face and shaking me so forcefully that he was hurting me. I was so scared. I told him to stop. I said "It's over; you crossed the line." "Let me go; it's over." I was literally trying to fight my way out of his tight grip on me.

I felt like a battered woman. I ran down the stairs to the waiting room where he sees patients and tried to escape out of that door. He blocked that. Then I said "I'll call the police if you won't let me go", but he still wouldn't budge. So I threatened to bring him to the licensing board and I finally made my escape onto the city streets. I walked very fast and as usual Dean was right behind me, following me. I was scared shit. I saw a police officer and I turned to him and said "this man has pushed me and is now following me". The police officer told me to keep going as he retained Dean.

I was quite shaken and called my husband to pick me up. He told me he wouldn't be able to come for a good forty-five minutes because he was taking our son home from his weekly visit. So I made my way into the old man's garage. I was lucky that he was there this time of night. I told him what happened. He already knew about my relationship with Dean. He never was thrilled about it and thought Dean was bad for me. He said "you can't drive a man over the edge; the next time he'll knock you across the head." Dean had called and left a voice message to talk to me. But I said this was it. Dean had crossed the line and became abusive. I was not going to be a battered woman!

After my husband took me home my son was extremely worried and concerned about my safety. I assured him that it was all over with Dean, that after what he did I would never, could never see him again. My husband and son were so relieved. They both agreed the next time it would probably be a slap in the face. I couldn't wait until the next day to see Dr. Love to let him know what happened.

Dr. Love agreed, from seeing abusive woman himself in therapy that physical abuse usually starts out the way it happened with Dean and then escalates into slapping and punches and then finally the woman is hospitalized and her own life is at risk. I told Dr. love that I broke up with Dean and that I was no longer going to do the couple's sessions. Dean wrote me another email and left another voice message on my cell phone apologizing. He just didn't get it that I was worried about his erratic and volatile

behaviors, that I was extremely worried
about my own safety!

Here is that "apology email':

Sandra,

 Sorry that you did not feel comfortable
attending the session this afternoon. I know
that that is on me...and, again, I can't tell
you how sorry I am for last night! I do really
hope that you can find your way at some
point to speaking to me about what had
happened...either with or without Dr. Love
present. I do still believe that it could really
make a difference...

I'm imploring you, Sandra, please give it a
chance...and don't let this be the last of our
relationship...

Dean

The next day I woke up with vengeance on
my mind. I told Dean that I was going to

report him to the board. He cried and pleaded with me not to. I was sweaty and disheveled from exercising and it was early in the morning before he started seeing his patients. I took off in my car in a fury and made my way over to his house. He was waiting for me on his front steps. I was furious. I screamed at him how much he hurt me. He apologized in tears and tried to hold me with his arms stretched out whimpering and pleading for me not to destroy him. He said he wanted to explain what happened.

He told me that every time I ran off out the door it reminded him of his mother. She use to give him the silent treatment for days on end not talking to him. Dean was feeling abandoned like he did as a boy. Dean' s mother was sadistic as well as his father. This I never knew. I knew he was badly beaten by his father but I didn't know he was emotionally abused by his mother. As punishment his mother would make him kneel on his knees in the corner for up to six hours until his father got home to beat him!

One time Dean saved up all of his money and bought his mother a ring. His mother looked at him with disgust and said "you think that is going to make things better." I was shocked by this news. I immediately felt intense sorrow for all that Dean had to endure that I put my arms around a sobbing Dean and held him tight. He told me that he felt so close to me at this moment. Our lips met and our tongues entwined in a passionate kiss as Dean was making his way under my tight exercise shirt. I had no bra on and he started caressing my breasts and playing with me nipples as he said "I wish we had more time." It was almost eight-thirty and Dean's first patient of the day was about to arrive!

Dean walked me out the door asking if I'll see him tomorrow night. I of course said yes. I wasn't too thrilled about going back to Dean after he abused me. My son was beyond upset and I got many lectures about being a battered woman and how I was putting myself in danger. I felt very shameful to have to hear this from my sixteen year old. Both my son and husband didn't like Dean and were very worried about my safety when I was with him.

Every night that I saw Dean my husband would say to me before I left "call me if you need me." The night that Dean abused me wasn't the first night that my husband had to come get me after Dean and I got into a fight. One time I ran off, called my husband and Dean followed me right to the public parking lot where I had my husband come to get me. In fact Dean and I were still arguing when I husband arrived! I got in the car and Dean just stood there looking at my husband with my husband looking back at him. I don't know if it gets any more bizarre in life than that!

So now there was transference of both parents onto me, Dean's mother and his father. And I had transference of my mother and sheer fear of abandonment placed on Dean. Dean still didn't know if he wanted a commitment with me or to live his life alone.

The torment of this whole situation was taking its toll on me. One day I decided to go over Dean's while he was in with a patient. I walked in the patient waiting room and opened the door that went up the stairs to his living space. I opened up his freezer where he kept the absolute vodka and made myself a martini. It was still early in the morning. I downed the martini down real fast, and made myself a second one. I was started to feel the alcohol kick in. I took, martini in hand and slowly ascended the stairway, holding my glass gingerly with one hand, and clutching the railing tightly with the other.

When I reached the top of the landing I headed around the corner, passing the bonsai plant, basking in the sun from the light of the window. It had its own special table, all to itself. Dean had many plants of different varieties and size, scattered through-out his home, even his bedroom.

I headed toward his office with my drink in tow. I started rummaging through his top drawer, feeling rather tipsy. I've been through this same drawer many times. But this time, to my complete horror I actually found something that I have never seen before.

I found a small receipt for a diamond ring, worth over eight thousand dollars!! I couldn't believe my eyes. Could this be real? I knew exactly what that meant. Dean was engaged, at some point. He had lied to me!! He told me he never was engaged or married, that he was a confirmed bachelor. The receipt was for jewelry store in Framingham. That's where his lawyer girlfriend lived! I also found a professional picture of them on a cruise. It looked like a honey-moon picture. It was taken in London. The date stamped on the photo was 2005. I heard a door close from downstairs. Den must have finished with his patient.

Dean was coming up the stairs. And as he was I sprang out of the desk chair like a frog placed in a hot frying pan filled with oil. I pushed the receipt right into his face as he entered the room. "So you were engaged" I said. "No, no I wasn't" he stammered. I asked "well what is this diamond receipt?" He kept swearing up and down that he was never engaged. But I knew differently.

I told him I was going to report his sorry ass to the licensing board for lying to me. I flew home in a rage, took out pen and paper and wrote a complaint to the licensing board for psychologists. I was devastated. How could he lie to my face after I already had evidence?

Not only did I mail a complaint, (something I was quite used to doing by now) I started looking in the phone book for lawyers. Yes, I was going to take legal action against him as well. Nobody, I repeat, nobody makes a fool out of me!

I found several lawyers names. And I made plenty of phone calls. Only a couple got back to me. They told me they wouldn't touch the case. One of them told me that he would look into it. This time no amount or pleading from Dean would change my mind! This was the last straw! Dean did try. Here is his pathetic attempt:

Sandra,

Please do not do this!   I am sorry that I had failed to disclose what I had not, but at first I thought it was irrelevant and over time as it felt like it was relevant, I wanted to tell you, over and again, but I became increasingly afraid of your vehemently jealous reactions to your perceptions about my former relationships and felt that that it would not serve any constructive purpose until we were in a better place together some day. I was just scared; that's all...

Dr. Love also reminded me in the session of you're having stated on numerous occasions that you would not go to the Board until you had spoken to him, just in case it was reactive; so, I am asking you to please do that before taking this action, which could be irreparable on so many levels!

Please allow us to have some kind of process around this together and\or with Dr. Love and\or with Bert!

Please...

Dean

Chapter 27 – The Demand Letter

One of the lawyers I contacted sent me an email explaining how a demand letter works and why it was in my best interest to pursue that first:

The legal system cannot put you back into the same position you were before all this happened to you, but what is can do is get you money as a substitute form of justice. So what I proposed are claims by which you can try to get money. If misrepresentations were made, then it is likely a violation of the G.L. c. 93A (the Consumer Protection Act). How much of a dollar demand I would put in the demand letter I can determine once I get the chronology and the all materials.

The Massachusetts statute, G.L. c. 93A (commonly called the Consumer Protection Act), is a powerful civil litigation tool if the Defendant committed an unfair or deceptive act or practice in violation of the CPA, because of the fact that the CPA requires a potential defendant who gets a certified mail demand letter pursuant to the CPA to evaluate the claims made in the demand letter at that time and then to tender a reasonable response within thirty (30) days of receipt of the demand letter. Many things violate the CPA, and most definitions of such violations are determined by courts in actual cases, but misrepresentations are one major category of CPA violations.

The potential defendant's failure to tender a reasonable settlement within the thirty days of receipt of the demand letter will result in the potential defendant being subject, after trial, to being required to pay the claimant's reasonable attorney fees, if, at the time of the trial, the court finds that the defendant failed to offer a reasonable settlement in response to that demand letter sent at the outset. The court can also impose a penalty of either double or treble damages for either that same failure to settle at the outset, or for egregious violations of the CPA, however, while the imposition of the multiple damages for the failure to offer a reasonable settlement or otherwise is unlikely, the payment of the attorney fees is mandatory if you win at trial. So the possibility of having to pay the claimant's attorney fees alone creates a strong incentive in a potential defendant who receives a demand letter to actually deal with trying to settle the claim when the demand letter is received, at the outset of the case.

If you put together a chronology that I can copy and paste into my demand letter, I am proposing to send a G.L. c. 93A (the Consumer Protection Act) demand letter, seeking a reasonable settlement. I would do that on a contingent fee agreement basis or an hourly fee agreement basis. I am probably not going to be willing to go beyond the demand letter stage and to file suit, however.

Please let me know if you have any questions.

I decided to go ahead with what the lawyer asked me to do. And he drew it up. Here it is:

I represent Sandra Wyllie. This letter is a demand letter upon you pursuant to the terms of Massachusetts General Laws c. 93A for your employment of unfair or deceptive acts or practices towards Sandra Wyllie.

FACTS

On 1/28/2012 Sandra Wyllie first obtained professional services, for psychological counseling, from you. She was seeing you once a week and you were billing her insurance, and she paid a $20.00 co-pay out of pocket as well.

On 5/19/2013 Sandra Wyllie had a three hour telephone conversation you initiated on a Sunday evening from 7-10 pm, that involved a dream you had in which she appeared. You related that in your dream you envisioned the two of you in your dimly lit office, with the lights low, and you described the setting as romantic. You then went on to say that you heard thunder in the sky and the sound of horses running by your window; that you took her over to your window and the two of you knelt down on the floor and saw the horses running by; that one of them stopped and looked directly at you; and the rest of that conversation was about your past girlfriends and your relationships.

On 6/25/13 you asked Sandra Wyllie to start coming for sessions twice a week. She did not have insurance, so you made an arrangement that she pay $45.00 out of pocket for each session.

On 8/6/13 you started physically holding Sandra Wyllie during the sessions. You would do this during every session, often swaying her in your arms, as if the two of you were dancing. You would hold Sandra Wyllie tightly to your body so that your bodies touched. This holding would last sometimes up to ten minutes.

On 9/20/13 you told Sandra Wyllie in a session that you had romantic feelings for her.

On 10/13/203 you asked Sandra Wyllie to start coming in on Sundays for therapy. At this point you dropped the session fee down to $20.00 a session. Sandra Wyllie was by then seeing you three times week. During most of those sessions you would discuss your own past abusive history with your father and your former relationships with your girlfriends.

On 11/29/13 you called Sandra Wyllie at 7:00 in the evening asking her to come to your office. It was after hours. When she entered your room it was dimly lit, and you took her over to your chair and sat her on your lap. You then placed your tongue inside her mouth.

On 1/1/14 Sandra Wyllie ended her therapy with you, as she felt that the relationship had ceased to be therapeutic. Instead, Sandra Wyllie started dating you, even though she was married and still living with her husband. You would drive to her house and pick her up, without coming inside. Your behavior greatly upset Sandra Wyllie's son, Austin, seeing his mother's psychologist pick her up for dates. The two of you then started a sexual relationship. The sex was mostly one-sided, with Sandra Wyllie giving you fellatio, but intercourse, while infrequent, did occur.

On 1/6/14 Sandra Wyllie gave to you the time for her session with her then therapist, Dr. Love, so you could start getting professional help. Then, you and Sandra Wyllie started doing "couples therapy" as well with Dr. Love. Dr. Love did not charge for you when you came during Sandra Wyllie's sessions. In the spring you started seeing Dr. Geist once a week on your own and then you finally paid.

On 9/7/14, while Sandra Wyllie was at your house you become violent with her. The two of you had an argument and she ran out the door. Whereupon you grabbed her and threw her on the couch and started shaking her and then you forcibly "pinned her down." She had her husband pick her up from your house, as her husband had done on numerous occasions when you and Sandra Wyllie would get into fights. Her husband worried about her safety.

On 11/12/14 Sandra Wyllie broke up with you for seven weeks, because she felt used in the relationship.

On 1/2/15 Sandra Wyllie contacted you asking to get back together with you, and the two of you resumed your relationship.

On 2/11/15 you started coming once a month with Sandra Wyllie to her new therapist Dr. Bert Lahr. And he billed Sandra Wyllie's insurance for the visits. You were still seeing Dr. love once a week, as was Sandra Wyllie too. The two of you would sometimes alternate doing "couples therapy" between Dr. love and Dr. Lahr.

On 2/24/16 Sandra Wyllie ended her relationship with you permanently, when she discovered you had lied about never being involved in a commitment, as you were engaged to another woman and were living with her. Sandra Wyllie's son, Austin, and her husband were getting emotionally more distraught over the relationship the two of you had maintained. You were hurting her whole family, and therefore she decided it was time to end to the relationship.

your inability to make a commitment. You swore you were "a loner" and had never committed to any woman before. Sandra Wyllie told you that she wanted a commitment that she did not want to keep having an affair.

On 2/24/16 Sandra Wyllie ended her relationship with you permanently, when she discovered you had lied about never being involved in a commitment, as you were engaged to another woman and were living with her. Sandra Wyllie's son, and her husband were getting emotionally more distraught over the relationship the two of you had maintained. You were hurting her whole family, and therefore she decided it was time to end to the relationship.

My lawyer set a price of $100,000. The demand letter was handed to Dean personally by the sheriff. I wish I could have been a fly on the wall when he received it! It didn't take Dean very long to agree to the demand letter. There was some small negotiating back and forth between our lawyers. In the end I received $80,000. But I had to give my lawyer $20,000 out of that.

Even my lawyer was amazed at the speed of the onset of the letter, which was in June to the final check cut, which was September! It was all behind me now. I felt justice was served.

I never did hear from the licensing board except that they were going to forward the case to prosecutions. But then there's always a chance Dean could appeal it, which would take more time.

Chapter 28 – Dean's Death

I was in a therapy session with my new shrink when he gave me the most devastating news of all about Dean. He said he found Dean's obituary in the Globe. I told him that I didn't believe him. He had to be wrong. He didn't know Dean's last name or what he looked like.

I asked him to go get the obituary. He went into his house and got it. Sure enough, it was Dean. The obit said he died unexpectedly. It was him alright, with his picture and profile. I stood up in shock, with the paper in my hand and started pacing back and forth. Dean was too young to die. And what did he die of? I wanted answers!

The only way to get the answers was to contact one of his closest friends. So I sent her an instant message. She was just as shocked as I was. She hadn't a clue that he had died. She also told me something else that was startling. Dean had been married!!!

I thought he just got engaged, and then broke it off!! He even lied about having a wife!! The whole relationship seemed to be built on lies. I would never trust anyone ever again, after this. This had destroyed me. I had nightmares after this. But I also felt responsible for Dean's death.

His friend told me he died of a heart attack. He just collapsed while he was at work. It was a patient who found him on the floor. His friend also told me that he was suffering severe stress from both his personal and professional life. I knew that I was the cause of that stress.

Although I thought Dean got what he deserved, he didn't deserve to die. At least he died doing what he loved the most, which was his work.

I've been through a hell of a ride. It has been the experience of a life-time. I learned a lot about transference and projection, old wounds that get acted on with new people in our lives, and why the law is there to protect patients from entering into sexual relationships with their psychologists. I learned a lot at such a high price.

And so did Dean.

Author's Page

My name is Sandra Wyllie. I've been writing poetry for the last seven years. I've been inspired by two great woman poets, Emily Dickenson and Anne Sexton. I also enjoy nature and photography. I've been published in Lucidity Poetry Journal, International and Ibbetson Street Magazine as well as having self-published many books available on Amazon, including "Life with my Schizophrenic Father" and "Looking for Mr. GoodShrink."

Made in the USA
San Bernardino, CA
27 September 2018